M000309644

GOT A MINUTE?

GOT A MINUTE?

SIXTY-SECOND EROTICA

EDITED BY
ALISON TYLER

CLEIS
PRESS

Copyright © 2007 by Alison Tyler.

All rights reserved. Except for brief passages quoted in newspaper, magazine, radio, or television reviews, no part of this book may be reproduced in any form or by any means, electronic or mechanical, including photocopying or recording, or by information storage or retrieval system, without permission in writing from the publisher.

Published in the United States by Cleis Press Inc., P.O. Box 14697, San Francisco, California 94114.

Printed in the United States.
Cover design: Scott Idleman
Cover photograph: Getty
Text design: Frank Wiedemann
Cleis Press logo art: Juana Alicia
First Edition.
10 9 8 7 6 5 4 3 2

"Swim" by Laura Marks previously appeared on www.cleansheets.com. "The Writer's Muse" by Gwen Masters previously appeared in *BUST* magazine. "What Kind of a Slut Are You, Anyway?" by N. T. Morley previously appeared in *Slut!* magazine. "Tasting Kate" by Jolie du Pré previously appeared on www.goodvibrations.com.

For SAM

Sex is a shortcut to everything.
—Anne Cumming

Love vanquishes time.
To lovers, a moment can be eternity,
eternity can be the tick of a clock.
—Mary Parrish

Contents

xi *Introduction*

1   *Flashers* • STEPHEN D. ROGERS
2   *Pink* • HELENA BLACK
5   *Squeaky Clean* • SHANNA GERMAIN
8   *A Quick Dip* • SASKIA WALKER
13 *The Other Side of Sleep* • MARIE POTOCZNY
15 *The Test* • XAN WEST
18 *His First* • NICK SANTA ROSA
24 *Hired Hunk* • RACHEL KRAMER BUSSEL
29 *French Postcards* • TERESA NOELLE ROBERTS
31 *The Rider* • CLARE MOORE
36 *Wake-Up Call* • AIMEE NICHOLS
40 *The Vague Language of Sex* •
    MICHAEL HEMMINGSON
43 *Every Night* • JEREMY EDWARDS
45 *Truck-Stop Quickie* • RAKELLE VALENCIA
49 *Case of the Hornys* • JOCELYN BRINGAS
55 *Hungry for Love* • SASKIA WALKER
58 *Swim* • LAURA MARKS
61 *What She Hath Deserved* • ALISON TYLER
67 *The Interior Virgin* • L. A. MISTRAL
72 *When My Boyfriend Is Away* • BROOKE STERN
75 *As She Was Told* • TENILLE BROWN
80 *The Perfect Season* • RACHEL KRAMER BUSSEL
84 *Muff Diver* • SHANNA GERMAIN
87 *Water Love* • J. SINCLAIRE
91 *Flying* • SASHA WHITE

94   *The Covers of Books* • MARIE POTOCZNY
96   *A River with Two Mouths* • STEPHEN D. ROGERS
98   *Marks, Reviewed* • DEBRA HYDE
101 *Tasting Kate* • JOLIE DU PRÉ
105 *Run-In* • TSAURAH LITZKY
110 *Fondue Night* • TERESA NOELLE ROBERTS
114 *Gloria* • JORDAN CASTILLO PRICE
119 *Perfect* • SHARON WACHSLER
123 *The Writer's Muse* • GWEN MASTERS
128 *Study Break* • JOLENE HUI
131 *A True Story* • CATE ROBERTSON
133 *From Bitter to Sweet* • ANDREA DALE
136 *Bart and Randi* • MICHAEL HEMMINGSON
139 *Pleasing* • JOCELYN BRINGAS
143 *Saturday Afternoon Steam* • JOEL A. NICHOLS
146 *The Magazine* • BONFILS
151 *How to Spank Me* • SHANNA GERMAIN
155 *Alley Obsession* • XAN WEST
159 *Watch and Wait* • JUSTUS ROUX
163 *Transformations* • JEN CROSS
168 *A No-Win Situation* • ALISON TYLER
172 *Holly's Fantasy* • KATE LAURIE
175 *Come from Behind* • CATE ROBERTSON
177 *Short-Lived Lace* • LYNN BURTON
180 *Salacious Robinson* • SYLVIA DAY
183 *Backroom Sally* • INGA MAHN
185 *She Lives Alone* • KATHRYN O'HALLORAN
187 *Research* • KATE VASSAR
191 *The Window* • AIMEE NICHOLS
194 *The Best Cure for Jet Lag* •
     TERESA NOELLE ROBERTS
198 *Nails* • BONNIE DEE

204   *Fencing with Discipline* • THEA HUTCHESON
208   *The Last Good-bye* • ALISON TYLER
213   *What Kind of a Slut Are You, Anyway?* •
        N. T. MORLEY
220   *On Your Back* • CATE ROBERTSON

221   *About the Editor*

| INTRODUCTION

Got a minute?

That's all I need...a minute.

Sixty seconds to grab your attention. To fasten your focus on what I have to say. Here's the truth: I've always had a thing for quickies. For those sexy, heart-pounding erotic encounters, when there's not even time to take down the panties, to kick off the faded denim. When a lover's fingers are on you, tearing satiny fabric aside, out of the way. When his mouth is against your neck, or her fingernails are gripping into your back. When there's hardly even time to whisper, to think, to breathe.

I have a thing for quick sex stories, as well. Capture my attention in the opening line, and I'm yours forever. Turn me on in fifty words or less, and I'll follow you home. I've written fan mail to authors who have pounded out an entire explicit story in a single paragraph, start to finish, prelude to climax. I am in awe.

It should be no surprise that my favorite personal ad I ever saw stated: *Man Seeks Woman*. So simple. So straightforward. So sexy. You can't get any more direct than that.

The following are sixty of the shortest—but by no means the sweetest—stories I've ever read, from some of the most talented writers in the business. An hour's worth of fiction from the likes of Saskia Walker, Rachel Kramer Bussel, Michael Hemmingson, Shanna Germain, and a slew of others. Each intense encounter is perfectly penned, and perfectly concise (from under seventy-five words to a maximum of fifteen hundred)—and destined to prove that a slow hand isn't always better. Sometimes throbbing and ferocious is what's truly needed to get the job done.

Alison Tyler
February 2007

FLASHERS

Stephen D. Rogers

In the half-light of dusk, they had the park to themselves. They wore matching raincoats and nothing else.

She stepped from behind a tree and flashed him.

He flashed her from behind a trellis.

Their bare skin glowed in short bursts, like two fireflies dancing around each other, until darkness fell and the two lovers finally met and joined on a bed of soft grass.

They took turns watching the stars blink to life.

PINK

Helena Black

From his place facedown on the floor, all he can see are her legs, the shimmery pink of her stockings, the dark shadows where the polish on her toenails peeks through. His hands want to travel the length of those stockings, higher and higher, moving against the softness of material on flesh. He can imagine his fingers creeping up her slender legs, tracing their way around that lacy rim snuggled tight against her pale thighs.

Earlier in the evening she had worn black nylons and now their scratchy-soft cat's tongue binds him, whispering at his wrists. He loves the slush-slushing sound they make when he tries to loosen their hold, a subtle reminder that he is hers.

He watches her legs as she walks around the room. She moves toward him and his cock strains even further, presses against the hard wood of the floor. He wiggles in a sorry attempt to relieve the pressure building there.

"Be still," she says, her voice a near growl. And he tries to argue but her approaching footsteps keep him in silence. She squats before him, gently patting his head, then purrs into his ear, "What a good boy you've been." He leans against her, lets her stockinged knees brush against his face. He can smell her there, that deep musky scent, and she opens her legs to him, allows his mouth a little room to explore.

He is on his knees now, kissing her thighs, biting at the tender flesh above her stockings and she opens her legs a little more, moves closer to his mouth. She is just out of reach, her hand covering her sex, and he watches as her fingers slide in and out of her warm, wet cunt. He nuzzles against her, tries to push past her hand with his tongue but she backs away from him, teases him more.

She changes hands, holds her glistening fingers out to him and he licks her fingertips, greedily sucking at her juices while the thumb of her other hand works at her swollen clit. Only when he's squirming and his cock is swollen and full does she open herself to him, giving him what he has been hungry for. His hot breath tickles the smooth skin of her pussy, and his tongue on her clit sends a sharp sting of pleasure. He sucks at her, biting her gently. His tongue plays against her as she continues working her fingers in and out of her cunt. She pushes them deep inside herself, then slides them into his mouth, reaches up to pull him closer, gently urging him on. He dips his head, replacing her fingers with his tongue, and she plays with her clit. They move back and forth between her cunt and her clit, her fingers and his tongue mingling with one another, taking turns. Her hips begin to buck with their rhythm and she grinds against him as she comes.

Her hands are in his hair now and she pulls him away, rolls him over and straddles him, sinks down onto his hard cock. Her stockings rub against his sides as she rides him, the nylons binding his wrists scratch his flesh raw in the small of his back.

She moves in tight little circles, his cock filling her. She plunges onto him, taking him in so deep, and he wants to come. His hips begin to buck beneath her but she pushes back. He is close to exploding when she suddenly stops. She presses down hard, still holding him inside her, but not allowing him to move. She stares at him for a moment and he can feel her cunt tightening around him. He tries to push into her but she slides off. She gets to her feet, stands looking down over him, her cunt dripping, a smile playing at the corner of her lips. Then, without a word, she turns and walks away. He tries to twist around, tries to see what she is doing behind him.

From his place on the floor all he can see is her pink retreat.

SQUEAKY CLEAN

Shanna Germain

There's something hot about washing sex toys. And it isn't just the water. There you are, standing at the sink, running your lathered hands up and down the bumpy blue shaft of your favorite vibrator, removing any signs of last night's play, leaving only memories. Beneath the soap and the water, the toy is almost alive, the way it shimmies and wiggles beneath the flow, a slippery fish headed upstream.

Flash back to last night: his hands, lubed, wrapped around the head, coming slowly down the shaft, preparing it for you. You can't remember wanting anything more, anything other than the quivering false-cock inside you, your lover's hands bringing it slowly, softly to the edge of your thigh, against your lips, forcing the tip inside as you arch your hips, moan, ask for it, please, yes, please. But he makes you wait, makes you beg before he slides it in, the rubber slipping deeper and deeper, whirring its quiet circles of pleasure inside you, filling you.

Your hands are rougher with the toy now, stronger as you

stroke the rubber, every last inch, making sure you don't miss a spot. The rubber is firm beneath your fingertips, and you close your eyes while you wash, imagining your hand around your lover's shaft in the shower, water raining on you both. Your hands soaped and slippery, sliding down and back up to circle the tip until he thrusts his hips against your curled fist.

You turn the vibrator on and it buzzes alive beneath your fingers, nosing in and out of your palm, searching for its flower, a scent of nectar. You set the toy—wet and humming—against the inside of your arm, and it makes your hips tingle and ache so that you press them against the edge of the sink.

You remember the mornings when he takes you before he showers. You, standing in front of the mirror, nearly swooning as he nibbles your neck before he bends you over the sink. He is quick and a little rough—the way you like it in the mornings—and your whole body seems to lift when he enters you, as though some invisible force is holding you aloft. He pinches your nipples until you look up at your reflection and the sight is enough to make you come.

The toy is clean now, but you can't help soaping it up one last time, just to hear the motor rumble as your palm runs up and down its length. After a few minutes, you reluctantly rinse the toy and turn off the water.

It's almost five and your lover will be home soon. You have a sudden image of meeting him at the door, toy in hand. No, instead you imagine draping your body across the couch, feet up along the armrest, vibrator sliding its way between your thighs.

Or you imagine him coming home, you calling out "I'm in here!" when he opens the door. He will come to the bathroom, find you elbow-deep in hot, soapy water, washing the blue vibrator that you used together last night. He will watch you run your hands along its thick shaft, and imagine it is his own cock, stiffening beneath your fingers. Then he will join you, pressing himself to your back, sinking his hands deep into the liquid next to yours.

You like this idea best, and you stand poised at the sink, the vibrator in your hand, waiting for him to enter.

A QUICK DIP

Saskia Walker

W hat would you say if I asked you out for a drink?" Gavin
gave her his best smile.

Adele chuckled, as if he'd said the very thing she wanted to
hear.

Once he'd seen her, this new girl manning the reception desk
at the gym, Gavin had made sure he dropped by for his workout during her shifts. They'd been teasing and flirting for over a
week. Tonight, he'd hung on until closing time, and on his way
out she'd flirted with him again.

Now, she leaned over the reception counter with her chest
squeezed against its hard surface. "I'd say yes. But…" She
glanced around. "There's nobody here apart from you and me,
and I'm about to lock up. Why don't we make the most of the
facilities, before we go for that drink?"

The way she said "facilities" made his cock hard.

She smiled as she stepped out from behind the reception desk and
walked over to the door, looking like the star of a wet dream. Her

sports top was ludicrously tight over her breasts; her shorts looked as if they had been painted on. She flipped back her shoulder-
length blonde hair and, after she clicked the lock shut, leaned her
back up against the door. "What will it be? A stiff workout in the
gym...?" Her eyes dropped to his belt. "Or would you prefer to
pound out a few lengths in the swimming pool?"

He eyed her body with interest. "Would you be wearing your
swimsuit?"

"Are you kidding?"

"That's what I was hoping to hear." He began to unbutton
his shirt.

"Race you," she challenged, tearing that tight sports shirt
up and over her head as she went, heading straight for the staff
entrance to the pool area.

Gavin followed, reaching the poolside just in time to see her
shorts being dropped and kicked aside. She was sturdily built,
with strong, rounded muscles and a shapely bottom that looked
like a juicy peach waiting to be bitten. She waved at him and
then her behind was displayed in its full glory as she bent over
to take a low dive into the water.

"Oh yes," he murmured, watching as her body flew across
the pool, a streak of warm, able flesh.

He stripped off, then dove in, covering the distance across
the pool with huge lunges.

"I do like a man who can spring into action when required,"
she commented, as he arrived at her side, shaking water from his
hair with a quick flick of his head.

"Then I'm your man," he grinned. He stroked her inner
thighs and she moaned in response. His chest rode up against
her pussy. He felt her flesh slide down his body as he stood up,
her shaved pussy coming to rest low on his abdomen. His cock
bounced up eagerly under her.

She drew in a lingering breath when his body applied pressure between her thighs. Her breasts bobbed in the water. He stroked them, his fingertips exploring the peaks of her nipples. He glanced down at the juncture of their bodies, wanting to push his cock home, but wanting to know how much she wanted it first. He thrust a finger inside her. She began to quiver and her arms grew rigid, pushing her upper body away from him. The water in the pool began to lap over her body as she twisted with pleasure.

"Give me your cock," she demanded. She was flushed, her eyes glazed with lust.

A dense thudding sensation started up at the base of his spine. He opened her up with two fingers and felt the sudden rush of water being sucked in against his cock as he probed inside her. The water gushed out again when he eased inside her cunt. She looked at him from beneath heavy lids, smiling appreciatively. "Oh, that's good, you fill me right up."

"Hold on tight," he rasped, hauling back. "I'm about to test your capacity."

She cried out when he thrust, her body arching to accommodate him. Their bodies seized together in the water, anchored by her arms gripping onto the side of the pool. He rose against her as he thrust deeper. She panted, forcing him to measure the thrusts while she rode them out. Waves began to spill over the edge of the pool. When he ran his thumb over her clit, she bucked, her cunt tightening on his cock. She let go of the poolside and gripped his shoulders, her fingernails biting into his back.

His physical responses were rapid, tripping wires all over his groin. "Jesus, I'm going to come," he muttered.

"Do me a favor," she breathed, in between his thrusts, "and look up at the camera when you do." She nodded over to where the CCTV camera overlooked the proceedings with a deviant expression in her eyes.

"Fuck," he said, glancing over from her to the camera that was trained on them. "You are one kinky girl." His blood was pumping ever harder, his cock rigid as he hit home deep inside her. He let loose a laugh, grinding his hips into hers, as he shook his head and grinned.

Her eyes were dark, her cheeks flushed, her wet hair slick. She loved what she was doing to him, lifting her eyebrows as she teased. "Oh yeah, I'll be watching you fuck me, over and over again."

"Jesus, you are bad, I'm going to show you just how bad." He hauled her legs in and latched them around his waist, grabbed her buttocks in his hands and shoved her up against the side of the pool, her back rising up against the tiles as he thrust her up and out of the water. He was seconds away. She held on to his shoulders, urging him on, delighted. Crying out, she squeezed him hard when he rammed deep inside her, roaring as he came.

He felt her begin to spasm. Her arms loosened their hold on him. Her sex clenched repeatedly on him, her body jerking in the water as she came.

"Do you do this with all your clients?" he panted, as his wet mouth sought hers and he steadied her as she found her feet.

She returned his kiss before replying. "Only the fittest, and you're it."

"Better keep coming back to work out, huh?"

"Oh yeah." She bit his earlobe, laughing softly as she slipped from his embrace and swam away toward the steps. "In the meantime how about that drink?"

"What about the footage?" He nodded back at the camera as he followed her and climbed out of the pool.

She smiled. "That's in case I want to take a quick dip," she winked, shoving her hand over her pussy and pushing her fingers inside, "when you're not around."

"Bad to the bone," he murmured, reaching over to slap her wet buttock.

She gave a blissful sigh, and shimmied.

THE OTHER SIDE OF SLEEP

Marie Potoczny

He says he loves the color of my skin. "Like toast," he whispers. He knows I am awake even though I am facing away, because I've shifted my breasts into a pretty pile rather than the spilling mess they are in when I'm asleep.

He kisses me high on my shoulder blades—my "wings" he calls them, which I love—and then brushes hair away to find my neck and ears. From the bottom of the house the coffeepot clicks on and begins to brew.

"You're such a golden orb," he says, trying to spur me on, testing to see if my waters run cool or warm this morning, and he slides his hand around my waist where it settles on my belly. I am happy here, in between sleeping and awake. There will be things to do today, pressing things, things that if I remind myself about, they would force me out of bed and away from him. But I choose not to remember what is on today's very important list of things to do and I fleetingly wonder again why I don't ever write, *Make Love* or *Orgasm* on the very top of my list of priorities.

"I know you're awake," he says.

I smile; I can't help but smile and then feign sleep, snore prettily, slightly tipsy, but tilt my hips for him to curl behind me. He reaches his other hand around in front of me, in between my legs, and I scissor them wide for him, wide for me.

"Don't wake me, I'm sleep groping," he whispers in my ear, "Never wake a sleep groper."

I laugh. Sleep laugh.

He pushes inside me and I hold my body still for him to find the hard bottom of penetration.

"Ah," he says.

"Ah," I say.

His fingers tickle my clit to the rhythm of his rocking. It is very quickly too urgent for kissing neck and shoulders now. And it is wet; there will be a wet spot on my side of the bed when we are finished, which will remind me to add laundry to the list of things to do, but not now. Now I forget for a little longer all the important things to do today, but not as important as this.

"Oh god," he says, and I know he is close because he always says *god* when he's close, and I love it when he comes inside me; thinking of him coming sends me off and I press his fingers in between my legs and hold them there to the rhythm of my orgasm, which is also the rhythm of his.

Our pleasure pulses and then recedes.

"Good morning," he says.

"Good morning," I say.

THE TEST

Xan West

'm pulled by my collar to the bathroom. You grab the hair at the back of my neck and push me to my knees. Your hand snakes over to lock the door. Now comes the test. You pull your cock out of your leathers, stroking it and looking down at me. My future, my pleasure, the fulfillment of desires long held hangs in the balance. Will I pass? Can I suck your cock well enough to convince you to take on a novice?

My senses are heightened by fear and desire. I knew the instant I saw you that I wanted you. Even *before* I saw you, I wanted you. Reading your ad made me hungry and nervous and wet. And now the test.

You are softly reminding me what is at stake, looking down at me, speaking seriously. It all turns me on: your words, the public nature of the situation, the test itself and the consequences attached to it. My skin is tingling, my face is flushed, and I'm already dripping wet. I look up at you, agreeing to the conditions you have set forth.

I grip you in my fist, tonguing the head, as I start stroking the base in slow steady thrusts. I take the head into the shallow of my mouth, coming down on it in time with my hand's movements. All the while I am hearing voices murmuring in the bathroom.

I move a little faster and take you into my throat. I keep this rhythm for a while, slowly sucking your cock in deeper with each thrust. My lips press down hard on your cock as I look up at you to find the exact amount of pressure you want.

"You love the feel of my cock in your mouth, don't you, slut? You've been thinking about this for days. It's consumed you. You've been imagining yourself on your knees, sucking me off. Come on, dirty slut, take all of my cock. Suck me harder. Like that. Faster. Take it all in. Show me what a good cocksucker you are."

The world disappears. All that's left is my mouth, your cock, and your words insinuating themselves into my pussy, grabbing my clit, pinching my nipples. My ass contracts as your words thrust themselves into me. I take your cock in deeper and harder, in time with the hard thrusts of your words. Your words urge me on, encourage me to open wider, take you in, thrust my mouth onto you, savor the feel of you in my throat.

My hand works your cock as I take you into my throat as far as you can go. I'm looking up at you through the tears in my eyes as my wet mouth engulfs your cock. Your hips are moving involuntarily, thrusting into my throat as you come. I take it all, shuddering on the brink of my own orgasm. I tongue your cock from the base to the head before I pull away and look up at you from my place on the floor.

My clit is throbbing. You look at me and stroke my hand. Then you grab the hair at the back of my neck and pull me to my feet. "On to the next test," you say. You pull me in for a kiss, thrusting your tongue into my mouth and biting my lip. Your mouth moves to my neck, tongues it fiercely and bites gently, then harder. "Later..." you murmur against my skin.

We exit the stall, your hand hooked in my belt leading me. I smile at the long line against the wall, and follow you out. I am completely unabashed about the time we have spent in there, despite the annoyance of those waiting, and walk out proudly. No shame in this slut. All I can wonder is...the next test?

What will the next test be?

HIS FIRST

Nick Santa Rosa

*H*er lips slip down my shaft one last time, her long brown
hair obscuring my view, but I feel the heat of her mouth
envelop me. She has a way of taking me all the way into her
throat and holding me there while I come, tongue massaging my
cock, coaxing me to my limits.

When I've finished, she lifts her head, and her tongue flicks
out to lick her lips. A smile creases her face. I still can't believe
she loves me.

Val: How do you do that?

Simone: Do what?

Val: Hold me in so long?

Simone: No one's ever done that before?

Val: Not like you.

*She tucks herself between my arm and chest, rests her head
on my shoulder and drapes one leg over mine.*

Simone: Oh, come on! All the women you've known, not one
deep-throated you?

Val: *All* the women?

Simone: Well, how many have you been with?

Val: This month…? Oww! That hurts.

Simone: Big baby. You pinch my nipples all the time.

Val: Not that hard.

She props herself on her elbows, her breasts dangling.

Simone: Tell me. How many?

Val: Seriously?

Simone: Seriously.

Val: Well, before you there was Lisa. Before her was Michelle. In college…

Simone: That's all? Just two since college?

Val: Counting you? Three.

Simone: Go on.

Val: In college I didn't date much. There was one girl at a party but I don't remember her name….

Simone: You had sex with a woman and you don't remember her name?

Val: I don't think I ever knew it.

Simone: Slut!

Val: Two-way street, babe.

Her breasts, partially obscured by hair falling in a cascade over her shoulders, sway slightly.

Simone: Who was your first?

Val: My first girlfriend?

Simone: Your first fuck.

Val: Darlyn.

Simone: How old were you?

Val: Eighteen.

Simone: How old was she?

Val: Seventeen.

Simone: Oooo. You could get in trouble for that.

Her breath is warm against my skin while she brushes her lips over my nipples.

Val: It was nothing special. Not very exciting, really.

Simone: Where'd you do it? In your car?

Val: No.

Simone: Come on. Tell me.

Val: You really want to know?

Simone: Yeah.

Val: Okay. It was Thanksgiving weekend. Friday, I think. The house was empty....

Simone: Your house or hers?

Val: Hers.

Simone: What was she wearing?

Val: Who's telling this story?

Simone: Sorry.

Val: T-shirt and jeans.

Simone: Bra and pant... Sorry.

Val: We were in her living room lying on the floor, talking and listening to music.

Simone: Like this?

Val: Not exactly. She was on her back and I was next to her, propped up on one arm.

Simone flops to her side of the bed, legs apart, waiting for me.

Val: Closer, but don't spread your legs. I usually started by pushing up her shirt and bra. I'd cup one of her breasts in my hand and kiss it, like this.

I demonstrate.

Simone: Did she have big tits?

Val: Yes.

Simone: Bigger than mine?

Val: Yes.

Simone: How big?

Val: Two handsful. I'd squeeze it a little to get her nipple closer to my mouth. Then I'd suck it...and flick it...with my tongue.

Simone: Would you bite it?

Val: Yes. I'd move back and forth between her breasts, not playing favorites. Then I'd slide one hand to her waist and slip it under the waistband of her pants.

Simone: Then she'd spread her legs for you?

Val: No. I'd get to her panties and reach under those, too. Touch her there.

Simone: Did she shave?

Val: No. She was seventeen and even more naïve than me. I'd always work slowly—I didn't want her to think I was in a big hurry to get to the main event.

Simone: You're a sly one.

Val: I'd grope between her legs and push them apart. Then slide a finger along her skin. Then two. Push one between the lips.

Simone: You did this a lot?

Val: Often. But, this time, I went for more.

Simone: *Wanna fuck?*

Val: Oh, no! Not so crass as that.

Simone: You didn't use that old "if you love me" line, did you?

Val: She wouldn't have gone for that. I just said, "I want to make love to you."

Simone: Just like that.

Val: Just like that.

Simone: *Yes! Oh, yes. Fuck me, baby!!*

Val: She was a little more reluctant.

Simone: You had to talk her into it?

Val: Kind of.

Simone: While you've got your finger up her pussy?

She squirms but plays along.

Simone: I'm not sure. Do you think we should? What if someone comes in?

Val: It'll be all right.

Simone: Well...I guess...okay.

Val: I pulled her pants off, and panties. Then I pulled my pants down....

Simone: You didn't take them off?

Val: No. She didn't look. Most of the time, when her eyes were open, they were on the ceiling.

Simone: Romantic.

Val: I guided my cock to her vagina...

Simone: Not her pussy?

Val: ...And pushed in as far as I could. Hers wasn't nearly as wet as yours.

It's a struggle to keep from sliding all the way in.

Val: I pushed in a little until I felt the friction of her skin, then pulled out, then pushed back in a little more.

Simone: Teasing her?

Val: Getting my cock covered with her moisture.

Simone: I want you.

Val: She didn't put her legs around me like that. Finally, when I was all the way in, I did what came naturally.

Simone: Fucked her brains out.

Val: Just slid in and out for a while...like this...until I felt myself...start to come...and just before...I pulled out...and came...on her stomach....

Simone: Oh, baby.

Her hand clutches my cock.

Simone: Oh, yeah. That's it. That's it, baby.

Val: Mmmm. I made a mess.

Simone: Now what?

Val: I pulled my pants up and got her something to clean up with. Probably a towel.

Simone: What a waste.

She pushes me to my back and settles herself back under my arm.

Her head rests on my chest. The evening comes in silence and I feel her breathing slow to a steady, sleepy rhythm.

Simone: I wish I'd been your first.

My hands smooth her hair and glide over her back.

Val: You are, baby. Every time.

HIRED HUNK

Rachel Kramer Bussel

I want to know what *really* turns you on. Where do you go in your mind when you come?" My girlfriend Dana's voice probed me with questions I was having trouble answering. Not because I didn't know exactly what I wanted, but because I wasn't sure how to tell her. We'd been together for three years already and when we'd first started going out, all her friends had warned her away from dating a bi girl. "She's trouble," they'd insisted, but I stuck in there. I knew Dana was the one for me, and I was right.

I'd never been as comfortable in my own skin, all-around horny, or happy in a relationship. But still, I had my fantasies, and the more she probed, the more they flitted through my mind. And yes, they involved a cock—but not in the way you might think. I wanted to watch a real live guy, a stud with a big cock, jerk off in front of us. Both Dana and I had taken to watching gay male porn we rented on more than a weekly basis from our local sex shop, and the minute the action started, we were all over each other. She'd never been with a guy, and after those initial conversations about who I'd dated and how I felt about them, she'd never wanted to know more than the basics. I had no idea how she'd react to the bombshell I was about to drop. But finally I caved.

"You want to know what I think about when I have my face in the pillow and the big vibrator going against me? I think about you and me wrapped around each other, hands everywhere, while some slick, shiny, stripper-type hunk slowly jerks off for us. I'm talking lube, pre-come, a grip so tight it looks like it hurts. I want to see him actually *rub one out.*" As I spoke, I could envision this luscious scenario in my mind, and I got so wet I had to touch myself.

"And then what?" she asked, a hard-to-read expression on her face.

"And then he comes, and we get our money shot, send him on his way, and fuck each other senseless."

"You just want to see him in the flesh? Nothing more?"

"He'll be our boy toy, our hired hunk. I know that it's crass and dirty but the thought just gets me so worked up."

"I've never even seen one up close before," she practically whispered, although we were alone.

I crawled across her, my body hovering over hers, as I fished out my favorite, totally unrealistic, shiny red dildo. Then I planted myself in front of her, straddling her body before slowly taking the head of the silicone toy in my mouth. I teased her with my stellar blow job skills until she snatched the toy away from me and, pounding me with it, made me cream all over.

I was assigned the task of finding Mr. Hunk, and I took my job seriously, staring hard at almost every guy I passed. Finally, I overheard some girls at work talking about a male friend, Tom, who hadn't had sex in over a year. He was climbing the walls.

"All he wants is to look at a woman at this point. He'll take what he can get."

I waited until the crowd had dispersed to inquire if he'd really just be content to *look* at a woman—or possibly two. I trusted Lauren with my secret—she's been a loyal friend forever. I whistled when she called Tom-the-hunk's photo up on her computer screen. He was shirtless, hair blowing in his face on the beach, and his muscles practically jumped off the screen at me. The faint outline of his dick was impressive too.

"We'll take him!" I proclaimed, as if I were at a male meat market.

"Let me ask him first," she laughed, but the next day, she confirmed that he was ready, willing, able and eager. "He thought it was too good to be true."

"Oh, it's true all right," I said, looking forward to speaking with him myself.

I liked making the plans, negotiating with Tom over just what he could and couldn't do. "But what if I want to kiss you? Or squeeze your breasts? Or lick you all over? I'm good!" he boasted. For the first time in ages I had the urge to throw a guy down and have my way with him. But that wasn't what our rendezvous was about.

I had been extremely curious about how he'd react to my butch girlfriend, but when we finally got together, they treated each other not like rivals, but equals, shaking hands proudly as they sized each other up, Dana wrapping one arm protectively around me.

We had him sit in our comfortable armchair while we got on the bed, huddling close. He didn't want any music on, so we just talked to him as he took off his clothes. "Show us your cock, Tom. We're dying to see if it's as big as we think it is,"

Dana said, getting even more into his show than I was. As he
took off his shirt, her hands moved down my sides, squeezing
my skin until she reached my hips, then pushed on. By the time
she got between my legs, I was halfway to orgasm. I'd never
truly thought I'd be in my bedroom with Dana and a naked
man at the same time, but within a few minutes, there was Tom,
stripped down and as hard as a rock. His impressive cock stood
proudly before us.

"Show us what you do at home," I said, licking my lips as I
sat up, getting on my hands and knees. He walked right up close
and then wrapped his hand around his dick and began sliding it
up and down. Dana instinctively handed me our bottle of lube.
Tom nodded a silent thanks, then let me squeeze some of the
cold, clear liquid into his palm. My gaze flicked from his cock
to his face as Dana began fingering me, adding more and more
until I felt stuffed full. "Yes," I squeaked, my voice high, the
way it only gets during sex, as Tom began beating off faster and
faster while her fingers slithered inside me, curling and pushing
and pressing and teasing. She knew just how turned on I was by
this forbidden, elusive glimpse.

"I want you to come at the same time," she said, her voice
stern but kind as she used her other hand to manipulate my clit.
I swallowed hard, restraining myself from asking for a taste of
the fat, gorgeous dick before me. I smiled at Tom—*Yes, she's
fucking me good*, my lips told him without speaking—and he
groaned, pumping harder and harder. We gave each other a series of looks until finally my head rolled back as Dana stopped
restraining herself in any way and simply slammed inside me. I
shut my eyes and surrendered myself to her touch, and I could
hear Tom coming, his breathing quickening and then subsiding.
When I opened my eyes, the room seemed to spin for a second as
I took in the bright lights and Tom's come all over his hands.

"You can kiss him—on the lips," Dana whispered in my ear, and so I did, while she hugged me tight, letting his lips part mine in one of the most passionate kisses of my life. Tom left soon thereafter and Dana kept me up most of the night, while in my head I relived that magical interlude again and again. Not many girls would be able to handle a minx like me, but thankfully, I've found someone who can more than keep up with my games.

Next time, I'm going to fulfill her biggest fantasy…. I just have to get her to tell me what it is first.

FRENCH POSTCARDS

Teresa Noelle Roberts

J ack drew the line at shaving his legs. Isabelle countered with black velvet stockings that belonged in a racy postcard from the 1890s, back when the pictures were all pale skin and voluptuous curves. Jack was pale enough, but he didn't have curves, even dressed in a black lace dress so short that his garter belt peeked out, high heels, and the velvet stockings. He was a tall, lanky young man transformed by costume and makeup into a willowy siren, neither boy nor girl. A wide black leather collar disguised his Adam's apple and lace-cuffed gloves softened his bony wrists, but hints of five o'clock shadow deliberately peeked through the makeup that Isabelle had applied. She left his long hair wild and curly.

Wearing a dress and stockings that matched his own, she put a leash on him and took him out dancing. She wore Docs instead of heels so that, short as she was, she appeared to be leading a beautifully ambiguous captive giant.

Then she brought him home and stripped off both his dress

and hers. A long-haired boy and a cropped-haired girl, each in a garter belt and black stockings. Hard cocks saluted between each pair of stocking-clad legs, but it was her purple silicone one that entered him that night, driving into him, moving against him, taking him over the edge.

They slept together in a heap of discarded velvet and lace, stained with makeup, lube and come.

THE RIDER

Clare Moore

D amn, she thought. By Pony Express company rules, the rider had only two minutes to dismount, throw the mailbag onto the other horse, mount up, and spur off.

She was alone at the station; her daddy was off to town. He'd be gone all day. But she'd been planning this for some time. It had to be a day when both her daddy was gone and her favorite rider was coming through.

This was that day.

Every time he came through, she thought about it. She watched him approach from the distance, coming closer and closer, then heard the heavy thumping rhythm of the galloping horse, and the commotion of horse, rider, and horse exchange. All in a heart-pounding flurry of an instant.

The rider was young, maybe eighteen, like her. And strong. With a slight moustache, a neckerchief that flowed out behind him, and a wide-brimmed white hat, pulled down tight on his brow. He was handsome. Not like most of the other riders who charged through her station, all timeworn and battered.

And he was polite. First it was "Ma'am" with a tip of his hat, each time, until she yelled out "Bess!" once as he galloped away. He gave a wave of acknowledgment. From then on it was always "Bess."

Then once, to her surprise and delight, after he quickly swung up into the saddle, he held tight on the horse's reins, leaned down, and placing his free hand on the thick of her long hair, he kissed her. Then he kicked the horse, and riding away, he turned in the saddle, smiling, and raised his hat.

The next time was her turn. She was wearing jeans and a plaid shirt, like always. But this time, just before her rider was due in, and after she looked quickly around to make sure her daddy was back in the barn, she unbuttoned the top three buttons of her shirt, and pulled the fabric open. She wasn't wearing anything else underneath. In her hand she grasped a folded-up note.

He came. Same as always. Through the trees, riding hard, into the station's yard. When he got up to her, he saw her open shirt, and her firm round breasts inside. He stared, almost tripping over himself when his boot hit the ground. He threw the mailbag up onto the other horse, turned to look into Bess's smiling and anxious face, then swung up into the other saddle.

"Here," she yelled, holding up the note. When he reached for it, she drew it back to her breast, forcing him to touch inside her shirt. He got hold of the note, and smiling, shook his head in amazement. Then he was off. She stood with her hands on her hips, watching her rider disappear in the cloud of dust. She heard him yell, and could just barely make him out, holding the note above his head with one hand and waving his hat with the other.

She buttoned up her shirt, and folded her arms tight up against her chest, her heart beating hard.

Now she was alone at the station; her daddy was off to town. This was the day. She had until 2:15.

First she went out to the barn, straightened it up as best she could, and on the new hay, in the empty stall, spread several bright print blankets. She hauled buckets of water in from the well, poured them into the wooden tub on the back porch, and took a long bath, scrubbing every inch of her body.

She went to the cabinet beside her bed, took out the treasured bottle of eau de toilette that had been her mother's, dabbed some on her neck and carefully between her breasts; then hesitantly and slowly, dabbed some between her thighs, then replaced the bottle.

She took her newly washed plaid shirt from the shelf, slipped it on, and stood before the cracked mirror. She fiddled with her long hair, first tying it back, then letting it out to flow over her shoulders and back. The watch on the table said 1:35.

Once more she stepped in front of the mirror, and unbuttoned her shirt. Pulling it open, she gazed at her young lean body; with her thin waist, tight stomach, and full breasts; then buttoned the shirt back up.

Another look at the watch. She grasped it in her fist, picked up her boots and jeans, and walked out the front door. From the porch, she looked toward the stand of trees, then toward the barn. She walked over to it, opened the doors, put hers boots in front of one door, and hung her jeans on a nail above the boots. She hitched the spare horse to the post near the door, then looked at the watch, and clinched her fist again.

She touched her neck where she had dabbed the perfume, then walked quickly back to the house, over to the cabinet, and again took out the small bottle. Another dab on her neck, and again between her breasts. She replaced the bottle and hurried back outside to the barn.

She stood in the shadows in the barn, just inside. Standing facing the open doors, she slowly unbuttoned all the buttons of her shirt and, gripping the watch, she closed her eyes. She could see her handwritten note in her mind: *Ride hard, knight of the desert. Claim your treasure, your reward. Your Bess.*

She knew he would be there for only an instant. By company rules, the rider had only two minutes to dismount, throw the mailbag onto the other horse, mount up, and spur off. She had to be fully ready for him. She held the watch in one hand. With the other, she felt her breasts, then slid her hand down over her quivering stomach, resting it between her thighs. She spread her legs, and slid her fingers inside, thinking of him and what was about to happen, and gingerly caressed herself.

She opened her eyes. In the distance, in the stand of trees, she saw the cloud of dust, then the figure on horseback. She stood straight, with her hands at her side. In an instant the rider was in the yard. Her heart was pounding. She watched from the darkness as the rider rode in, and pulled his horse up. She tensed as her rider let the reins fall, then turned to the barn and quickly walked toward it. He stopped, and lowered his head to shade his eyes with his wide brimmed white hat. Then he saw her.

He continued his walk, and stood before her. He gently pulled her shirt open. Impatient, she dropped the watch and quickly grabbed his belt and unlatched it, and his jeans, and his underclothes, just as she had rehearsed in her mind many times at night in bed. Her aggressiveness seemed to remind him of the urgency of the situation, and he grabbed her breasts hungrily with both hands. His body had already responded, and came out hard through his unbuttoned underclothes, held by her stroking hands.

With a firm but gentle grip, she pulled him toward her as she backed up to the blankets. Never letting go, she sat down, then lay back, still pulling him, then guiding him between her thighs, into her open and wet self. Then she released him. He drove himself in the rest of the way, but held himself up so he could watch her face, with her eyes closed and mouth open and gasping, as he repeated his accelerated thrusts.

She grabbed his wrists, and met his rhythm until at last he burst inside her, filling her with an excitement and warmth she had not experienced before.

When she let go of his wrists, her hand found the dropped watch. "Rider," she said, holding up the watch in front of him. He stood to his feet, put himself together, buckled his belt, and looked down at Bess, still lying on the blankets on the hay with her shirt open, her firm breasts heaving atop her panting chest.

The rider tilted his wide-brimmed white hat. "Bess," was all he said, then turned and left the shadows of the barn. She propped herself up on her elbows and watched as he picked up the mailbag, mounted the horse, and spurred it away.

She watched as he raised his hat in farewell, then she lay back and fell asleep, to dream of knights in the desert.

WAKE-UP CALL

Aimee Nichols

Emma stared longingly at the phone on the counter in front of her. Around her, the early afternoon shoppers milled about the department store's various counters, thankfully not approaching hers. She was far too distracted to harp on the virtues of night replenishing cream. Every cell in her body ached to pick up the phone and ring Lana. She needed to have that honey-and-gravel voice ricocheting through her head again. Lana invaded Emma's thoughts to such an extent she was rendered useless, standing there at work staring fixedly at the phone as if awaiting a call from God.

Two months ago she would have scoffed if anyone had said she would feel this way, but two months ago *Lana* was just a name her friends mentioned sometimes.

The phone rang, jarring Emma's nerves and sending her heart pounding.

"Good afternoon, Ashton's beauty department. Emma speaking."

The voice that responded was more acid-and-metal than honey-and-gravel, and it enquired after some imported cleansing lotion. Emma dealt with the query and hung up, surprised by the resentment she felt toward the customer for not being Lana.

That was it. There was no point denying the urge to make the phone call; her need was not going to simply go away by itself. She glanced around surreptitiously; no one was heading for her counter, so she picked up the receiver and dialed Lana's number.

"Hello?" The voice sounded huskier than usual.

"I'm ringing from work."

"Hi, honey," Lana answered lazily. "You woke me up. I was just in the middle of a wonderful dream where I was Angelina Jolie's erotic maidservant. I seem to recall a lot of knives."

"Sorry," Emma murmured. "I thought you'd be up by now."

"It's all right, baby. What can I do for you?" Emma felt a jolt go straight to her clit, and her nipples hardened under her white cotton bra and regulation crisp white shirt. She crossed her free arm over her chest, certain people would notice. This was totally wrong. If anyone even suspected what she was about to do, she'd be fired on the spot. "I was hoping you'd play with me," she whispered into the mouthpiece. "I can't stop thinking about your body, and the thought of fucking you is making my knickers wet. They're sensible cotton knickers, the type my mother would approve of. Except I don't think she'd approve of this."

She was rewarded with a throaty laugh.

"That's delicious. I can see you clearly now; the eager-to-please baby dyke beauty consultant with a head full of dirty thoughts and panties full of juice. What would your rich, middle-aged customers think if they knew you were a raving pervert?"

Emma was warming to the game. There was an unadulterated thrill in watching people wander past oblivious to her arousal.

"They'd probably be excited," she said. "Maybe it'd let loose all those fantasies they hide away behind their bridge club and hair appointments."

"Or maybe they'd think you're a dirty slut."

"I'm *definitely* a dirty slut when I climb onto your lap and start kissing you, running my fingers through your hair and pressing against your stomach, grinding against you so you can feel how turned on I get just from being near you."

Emma heard Lana catch her breath, and allowed herself a smile that was one part triumph and three parts arousal. "I like to tangle my fingers in your long red hair, then close my fist around a handful and yank it so your head snaps back and your eyes widen in surprise. You're even more beautiful when you're immobilized and don't know what to expect, you know that? Your throat's exposed, and I understand vampirism completely when I kiss and suck and bite your translucent skin, leaving pale red marks that slowly fade as I turn my attention to your breasts."

Lana moaned, softly but tellingly. Emma imagined her sitting on the side of her bed, legs apart, pressing the receiver to her ear with one hand and touching herself with the other. Her breathing became harsh and jagged at the thought, but she worked hard to control herself, doing her best to make it look as if she were simply dealing with another customer's routine beauty requests.

"I raise your breasts, soft and full, and stroke your nipples with my thumbs. They respond wonderfully, hardening and extending."

"Suck them," Lana moaned. "Suck my nipples."

Lana began to pant heavily, and Emma pictured her rubbing herself into a frenzy, ready to come at any moment. She knew what would get her there.

"I'm going to lick your cunt, Lana."

She heard a sharp intake of breath.

"I climb off your lap and you watch me like a hawk, unsure

of what I'm going to do, but hoping all the same. I spread your legs and lie between them, breathing lightly on your pussy. You tremble and tilt your head back. I start caressing you with my tongue, savoring your taste and silkiness."

Emma paused to hear Lana's breathing and the little moans that escaped her mouth without her realizing. Emma's own breathing hammered in time with Lana's, and she turned her back on the store to give herself as much privacy as possible.

"You writhe against me and I gather your clit in my mouth and suck it hard."

"I'm gonna come!" Lana gasped, and immediately let out a series of moans. Emma could hear her thrashing on the bed. She waited, still with her back to the store, for Lana to recover.

"That was wonderful," Lana murmured when she had her breath back.

Emma smiled. "Glad you enjoyed yourself. But I should go. I don't want to get sprung for making personal calls during work time. Especially not *this* personal."

Lana laughed and they said their good-byes. Emma hung up and stood leaning dizzily against the counter. Her cunt cried out for release. She licked her lips and ran her mind over the conversation, considering what tonight's visit with Lana might bring.

Unconsciously, her hand moved to the front of her skirt and pressed in against herself. She could just manage to stimulate her clit. She let out a small moan.

"Excuse me?" said a voice behind her. She jumped and turned to see an impatient-looking woman at the counter. The woman's gaze met hers knowingly as she asked to try some moisturizer.

Oh god, what had she heard?

THE VAGUE LANGUAGE OF SEX

Michael Hemmingson

Nick had been waiting for Shella to leave her husband all summer; now that she'd done so, and she had her own apartment, she called him on the phone and said, "Why don't we go out?"

"How's your new apartment?"

"Come over and take a look," Shella said.

The place was spare when he arrived. There were a lot of unopened boxes.

Shella was wearing black jeans and a white tank top. Her hair was messy; she looked like she had just woken up.

"I took a short nap," she said, pointing to the couch.

"Naps are good," he said. "This is a nice apartment."

A jet flew over, heading for the airport.

Shella winced. "Now you know why the rent is cheap."

"You'll get used to it."

"Come see the view over here," she said. She pulled at his sleeve. They went to the bedroom. She had a view of the airport and the bay. The sun was setting. It was the end of summer; the ends of summers were always good in San Diego.

They stood on the small balcony.

More jets landed at the airport. Some took off. Sailboats, yachts and cruise boats lingered in the bay.

"Nice," Nick said.

They went back inside.

"And here's the bed," she said. The bed was unmade; there were three big pillows on it.

"Nice."

She pushed some of her dark hair from her eyes and said, "Okay, Nick, look, we like each other, there's chemistry, so why don't we just get it over with? Why don't we just fuck right now and get it out of the way?"

"All right."

They didn't kiss. She didn't want to kiss. Shella took off her jeans and panties and lay down on her stomach. She put a pillow under her pussy and raised her ass in the air. Nick wondered if she wanted it in the ass but her asshole didn't look like it had ever been fucked. Her asscheeks were round and skinny and pale. He took off his jeans and underwear, moved behind her, and slipped his cock into her cunt. She gasped and he grabbed some of her dark hair and yanked on it, pulling her neck back.

"Oh yeah," she said.

"Yeah."

"Fuck me," she said.

"I'm fucking you."

When they were done, they put their underwear and pants back on and went to dinner at a steakhouse downtown. They sat in a booth and sipped martinis and waited for their food.

"This is one of my favorite restaurants," Shella said.

"It's a nice place," Nick said.

During the course of the night, they were approached by two couples who said "Hi, how are you?" and gave Nick strange looks. Both couples were friends of her husband's, she told him. "Soon to be ex-husband," she said.

"Do they know that?"

"I don't think they know Jeff and I are separated."

"That's why they're looking at us—me—funny," Nick said.

"The heck with them," Shella giggled. She was enjoying the martinis.

They were fairly drunk when they returned to her apartment. They had some vodka tonics and got drunker. They sat in front of her TV and kissed, then she moved her head down and gave him a blow job.

It was a good, sloppy, wet blow job. "Your teeth," he said a couple of times, and she giggled as he pushed her head back down. He came in her mouth and she sat up and smiled at him.

"Was that nice?" she asked.

"That was nice," he said.

"We should do this again," she said.

"I'd like that," he said.

She didn't want him to stay the night. She said she wasn't ready for that. Nick understood.

They didn't kiss goodnight.

They shook hands.

EVERY NIGHT

Jeremy Edwards

She calls them her "ass pajamas," and they are identical—in every respect but one—to her other pair of pajamas. Each set consists of a skintight cotton jersey with matching bottoms— almost like long johns, but without ribbing. Each set is the same solid color, a vivid raspberry-sherbet pink.

But she has modified one pair—adroitly cut and hemmed it—so that the bottoms have no seat. From the front, I cannot tell which pajamas she's wearing.

Every night, she goes upstairs and gets ready for bed, while I finish the dinner dishes. We both know that her sex drive is not as high as mine, and that whether or not she will be in the mood is a matter of chance.

Every night, I enter the room and find her sitting up in bed reading, in raspberry-sherbet pajamas, the covers pulled up to her waist. Every night, she gives me a tender smile, puts her book down, and scoots under the covers until she is lying flat, faceup, on the bed. She closes her eyes.

Every night, I greet her in bed and kiss the thick, smiling lips that echo, in more muted tones, the hue of her pajamas. Then I pull the covers down just beyond her bare feet. She looks good enough to eat in her sorbet-smooth second skin, her fresh, loving face framed by a page-boy shell of chestnut hair that sinks listlessly into her pillow.

We do not want her to have to tell me, in so many words, "I want to be fucked tonight," or "I do not want to be fucked tonight." And so, every night, I simply reach a hand under her ass. This is what she and I have arranged.

If I feel the seat of her ordinary pajama bottoms, then I kiss her again, I pull the covers up to her chin, I whisper goodnight... and I pad off to the bathroom to handle my own libido.

But if I feel the frank immediacy of her bare ass, then I know that she is inviting the squeezing of cheeks and the tickling of the space between them. That she is longing to be rolled over, so that her derriere may be attended to with fleshy kisses and gentle, delicate little slaps. That she is counting on me to caress and cajole her naked bottom until her raspberry-sherbet crotch darkens with moisture and her raspberry-sherbet legs spasm and kick with uncontainable delight.

That she wants to feel the taut rib within my own pajama bottoms, as I press down upon her radiant, jiggling cheeks, and flatten them ever so slightly with my weight.

And we both know that before we sleep we will merge, stripped and torrid. That we will fuck with a frenzy that makes the house seem to vibrate, as it does when the washing machine spins its ass off on a Sunday afternoon. That we will shriek our ecstasies like the enamel teakettle—which rests quietly now, downstairs, in the kitchen that I tidied up while she was choosing her pajamas.

TRUCK-STOP QUICKIE

Rakelle Valencia

A sharp but not unpleasant pain brought her senses into acute focus. Teeth bit her flesh at the crook between neck and shoulder. She knew her skin would brighten red under the nipping and suckling insistence. Her body shuddered, involuntarily pulling at her wrists. The hand around them tightened.

Their eyes had met in the parking lot. Usually, she never looked anyone in the eye. Out on the road a person had to be careful, especially at these rest stops. Especially alone. Women truckers weren't that prevalent, and they weren't that well liked by the men trucking, except as potential bed companions.

So she rarely looked up while rushing to or from the ladies' room. But this time she had. And when their eyes had met, there was an electric energy; an excitement through her entire body. She couldn't stop staring. The woman was tall and lanky and handsome. Her own short, quick steps had unintentionally caught up to the woman's long, moseying strides across the back lot where the big rigs were parked. Their eyes had met and held, too long. That's how they both ended up in her sleeper cab.

Her shirt had been discarded along with her bra, and her wrists were now being held in a tight one-handed grip behind her back. The position of kneeling on her bed with her hands low behind her had thrust her chest forward and upward. Her skin tingled with life; a walking shell just awakened.

A hand cupped one of her breasts as a mouth descended on her nipple. The mouth was hungry, and she knew this one nipple of hers would never be enough. The woman's hand left her breast to slide flat along her stomach, resting a moment in the middle, warm and erotic. When the woman continued downward with her hand, it was to release the snap on her jeans and draw the zipper open so slowly, *too* slowly. Then long, lanky fingers slid under the waistband of her panties. And she gasped.

Wetness had already dampened the crotch of her panties; wetness she hadn't expected. Even during masturbation she would always resort to using lube. But those lanky fingers had found her soaked and wanting. They stroked the crease between her lips, up and down, excruciatingly slowly, drawing moisture over her clit, which made her jump and writhe. The handsome woman said nothing. Her mouth roamed between breasts and stomach, then to her collarbone again, her shoulder and her neck, before taking her lips prisoner, much like her wrists.

At first, the stranger had teased her mouth, plucking her lower lip, sucking it in to release it, nipping it slightly, then encouraging her tongue into play, all before the woman devoured her mouth. Tongues tangled and twisted, touching lightly and tentatively before aggressively taking what each needed. Lips smashed against each other, pinched by teeth. And all the while, two long slow stroking fingers strummed her to exquisite heights.

Her hips shoved forward, pleading in a carnal fashion. But the slow-moving fingers continued at their own maddening pace.

She bucked a few times because the flesh was taut and eager and wanton.

The woman then penetrated her with those two fingers, using the thumb to continue the slow stroking. Their mouths came apart. She halfheartedly made an attempt to free her wrists without success. Then she felt the assault to her nipples. Lips pulled at each in turn. Teeth nipped, then bit. A tiny squeal was released from her throat, making the woman cover her mouth once again in a dance of tongues.

Fingers inside her pounded a harder rhythm. The woman's thumb moved into the motion of rough little circles, first over the clit shaft then down the clit, back up, then down again, never breaking from perfect circles.

She cried out. The sound caught in her mouth and in her throat as if smothered by the handsome woman's mouth, her lips, her tongue. She cried out until her throat filled with screams that went unheard outside of her cab. And her screams came in spasms. They came in the same spasms that racked her body in undulating waves, clenching and unclenching on the woman's two fingers while pushing and shoving harder against that circling thumb.

Tears escaped her closed eyes. Rivulets ran the length of her cheeks in their own abandonment. Her screams turned to cries then to a soft mewling as her body wanted to collapse but was held upright by her imprisoned wrists.

When she awoke to find herself alone, she didn't remember quite how that had happened. Her body lay crumpled in a half-naked heap on her bed. Leopard spots dotted her torso, and she rubbed at the redness of her wrists. But the lanky, handsome woman was gone.

She quickly ran fingers through her rumpled, shoulder-length hair, yanked on a T-shirt and fought her way from the sleeper cab into the darkening evening. Briskly, she walked to the middle of the lot and turned a full circle, looking, hoping.

But the woman was nowhere to be seen.

CASE OF THE HORNYS

Jocelyn Bringas

G ene Douglas stared at his cock and groaned in frustration. He had been hard the whole day and it was beginning to irritate him. Nothing he did could make it go down. Earlier he had fucked a chick he met at Club Element and come three times. He already tried jerking off but it only made him harder.

For the past few weeks, Gene had felt more sexually charged than normal. It was fun at first because he felt he had gained more stamina. The women he fucked appreciated his willingness and were amazed at how many times he could come.

Gene thought he was on top of the world and that no porn star could match his sexual power. It wasn't until he noticed people pointing and staring at him that Gene realized something was wrong. He'd looked down and seen a huge tent in the crotch of his pants. He hadn't even been aware that he had an erection. It was very embarrassing to have an erection in public. He didn't want to walk around being classified as a pervert. He thought the solution would be to have more sex. Every night after work, he would head over to Club Element and pick up random chicks to fuck. Still, later that evening, he would find himself lying in bed with a throbbing cock craving more stimulation.

It was time for Gene to seek professional help, he realized. Logging onto the Internet, he searched for the perfect doctor to help him. He stumbled across the website for Dr. Cadence Parker, a board-certified sex therapist, and decided to arrange an appointment.

Dr. Parker's clinic was not like any other clinic Gene had visited before. On the outside it looked to be a very conservative place, but the interior revealed a drastic change in setting. The walls were covered with explicit pictures of different people in various sex positions. The chairs had certain parts shaped out of sex organs. Various sex toys were scattered around as decoration. On the waiting room tables were stacks of hard-core porn magazines. A porn movie was playing on the TV, from which loud moans were echoing throughout the office.

"May I help you?" a soft female voice said.

Looking in the direction of the voice, Gene saw a woman sitting behind a desk.

"I'm Gene Douglas. I have an appointment with Dr. Parker," Gene said hesitantly.

"She'll be right with you in a few minutes, feel free to have a seat."

As he sat down, Gene noted without surprise that he had an erection. He picked up a magazine and flipped through it. His cock throbbed even more as he gazed at the obscene images. Since Gene was the only person in the waiting room and the secretary was busy typing away on the computer, he nonchalantly placed the palm of his hand over his crotch. He gently rubbed himself as he imagined fucking all the women on the page he was looking at.

"Gene Douglas?"

He quickly closed the magazine. A blush crept to his cheeks and he stood up.

"That's me," Gene said.

"Mr. Douglas, I'm Dr. Parker. Right this way," Dr. Parker said, gesturing ahead as they walked toward her office. Dr. Parker was dressed extremely conservatively in a pantsuit.

"Have a seat right there," Dr. Parker said as she went to sit behind her desk.

Gene looked around and noticed she had an extensive book collection. On the wall behind her, he saw her various university diplomas.

"What brings you here, Mr. Douglas?" Dr. Parker asked.

"I think I have a problem."

"A problem with what?"

"My penis. It gets hard when I don't want it to."

"That's normal."

"Yeah, but I'll be out in public and then BAM! It's just up. People point and stare."

"Is that why your hands are on the front of your pants now?"

Gene blushed.

"Are you currently taking any medication?"

"None at all. All this started a few weeks ago and I thought it was cool, you know? I was fucking all these women and lasting longer. It was awesome until recently. Now I'm just hard all the time and it's not fun anymore."

"Well, what I'm going to do is obtain a sperm sample from you and run some tests. I should be able to make a diagnosis when I see the results."

"Okay."

"I'm going to ask you to go into the room across the hall and one of my nurses will be with you shortly to help."

While Gene was in the room waiting for the nurse, he couldn't resist starting to masturbate. Turning on the TV, he watched as the porno began to unfold. He thought he could conceal his masturbating with the long shirt he was wearing if the nurse walked in.

Unfortunately, the nurse walked in quite abruptly, without so much as knocking. The busty young brunette seemed to be immediately hypnotized by his cock. After closing the door behind her, she dropped to her knees and engulfed his stiff cock between her cherry-red lips. Leaning his head back, Gene relished the pleasure the nurse was giving him.

"Baby, I'm gonna come," Gene moaned.

Without taking her lips off his cock, the nurse reached for a tube. Once Gene started to orgasm, she placed the tube on his hardness and finished jerking him off. He watched in fascination as his sperm began to fill the tube. Panting, Gene saw his cock was still hard. Before the nurse could leave, he pulled her onto his lap and fucked her.

A few days later, Gene was back at Dr. Parker's clinic, anxious to find out the results of the tests.

"Hello, Mr. Douglas," Dr. Parker said as she walked into the waiting room.

Gene's eyes bulged out of their sockets the moment he saw Dr. Parker. She was bare naked.

"Hi, Dr. Parker," Gene said shyly.

Gene couldn't help checking out her voluptuous body as they walked to her office. Dr. Parker had a very nice ass that jiggled each time she took a step. Explicit thoughts began to run around in his mind and he began to get an aggressive erection.

"I checked out your test results, Mr. Douglas."

"What's wrong with me?"

"It seems you have a severe case of the hornys."

"I do?"

"It explains your excessive need for sexual pleasure as well as your experiencing unwanted erections. As of right now, I can only tell you that research is being conducted in search of a cure."

"So I guess I'm stuck with this for a while," Gene said, pouting.

"Yes, but in the meantime, I can help you out temporarily with some treatment."

"Really? How?"

Dr. Parker stood up and walked toward Gene, who licked his lips in anticipation as his eyes roamed over her curvaceous body. She sat on his lap, causing him to groan in pleasure when he felt her pussy pressing down on his hard cock.

"I saw you fucking Nurse Kandi the last time you were here. Now it's my turn," she whispered in his ear.

Her manicured fingers grabbed his shaggy blond hair and pulled him forward for a passionate kiss. He kissed her back fiercely for a few moments before pushing her off his lap and quickly shoving down his pants.

Dr. Parker then bent over her desk, offering her round ass to Gene. He wasted no time in sliding his cock into her pulsing pussy. The sounds of hard fucking echoed throughout her office.

"I could definitely get used to this treatment," Gene said, as he pounded into her.

Gene ended up fucking the doctor all over her office. It was the first of many fucks he and Dr. Parker shared. Currently, no cure has been discovered for patients who experience a case of the hornys. However, through the help of Dr. Parker and her various nurses, Gene has learned how to deal with his issue.

HUNGRY FOR LOVE

Saskia Walker

'm so hungry for you. We flirt across the restaurant table and our food, while I sit there thinking about what we're going to do when we're finally alone. It's a favorite pastime of mine, but you know that, don't you? And you love every minute of it because it gets me so wet. In fact, you'll find out just how wet it's getting me when you touch me there, later.

You watch me eat—your direct, observant stare sending a shiver of anticipation under my skin. The electricity crackles between us. I idle over mental images of your naked body while I imagine how you'll use it tonight. Your hand moves to your wineglass, and I watch and wonder if that hand will cup my naked buttock as you ease me onto your erect cock. I can almost feel your chest, pressed against my naked breasts. I'm very wet now; my panties are cleaving to the groove of my sex. If you could feel that, would you savor it, or ram your cock home? I rearrange myself on the chair, aching with need. The movement catches your attention. You look directly at me again, an accusing glint in your eye.

My pulse rate nudges higher. I speculate some more, knowing that you're observing me even more closely. With one finger, I trace the line of my shirt where it dips into my cleavage, your eyes following. Will you suck my tits and explore my sex with your fingers? Will you undress me slowly, observantly, or barely bother to take anything off? What would you do if I said I wanted that?

I've given up eating. How hungry will I be for you by the time we get to each other? How loud will you moan when I go down on your cock?

You fold your napkin. You refuse the dessert menu, asking for the bill instead.

I'm thrilled.

You whisper that I look as if butter wouldn't melt in my mouth, but you're willing to bet it'll melt elsewhere.

I like your suggestion for dessert. I smile and stand up.

You grasp me against you as we leave, your hand sliding possessively around my hip.

My heart races as our time alone draws near. Will you beg me to sit on your face while I give you head? Will you lead me to bed, or have me fast and furious up against the wall, my skirt up around my waist, my panties hanging on one ankle? Or better still, will you turn me around and bend me over a chair, giving me your cock hard to quickly relieve this fast-growing tension between us? How will you react when I tell you what it's doing to me? And you know that I will tell you, loud and dirty. I'll ask you to fuck me harder, if I want it that way.

Outside the restaurant, you turn into a dark alleyway and snatch me against you, kissing me hot and hard, your tongue thrusting into my mouth, your hand under my skirt, backing me against the wall.

You groan and murmur admonishments when you feel my

wetness, your fingers delving into my black lace panties to explore me.

God, that's good.

Hauling your hand out, you taste me and then tell me to turn around and lean up against the wall. When I do, you nudge my legs further apart with one powerful knee.

I shudder, my legs weak with desire.

You tell me how dirty I am, you tell me that you could see what I was thinking a mile off. You ask me how you were supposed to enjoy your food with this horny slut creaming her seat in front of you.

I shake my head, my body flushed with heat, my hips arching back, inviting you in. I hear your zipper; feel your cock nudging against me.

I'm on fire for it.

You strip my panties down my thighs. You ask me again, you want to hear me say it aloud.

I tell you that I was hungry most of all for love.

You lift my hips, feeding me a length of your cock, asking me yet again, knowing I'm desperate.

I cry out for your cock, begging you to give it to me.

You ram home, filling me to overflowing, quickly surging into me over and over again.

I come moments later, my body shoved up against the wall with the force of your attack. I cry out in sheer bliss, the sound echoing around the dark alley.

You whisper in my ear that this dessert option will have you coming back again. You say you intend to take a portion home.

I smile, clutch you against me and tell you I'm glad, because my hunger for this only seems to grow.

SWIM

Laura Marks

watch the sun licking other bodies through the water. The light
is like kisses trailing my body, covering my arms, discovering
the curve of my neck, rolling over me as I arch my back, twining
around my legs; patterns of light, lines of bright white against
blue water, tumbling between my legs; tongues like flames exciting me, propelling me forward, then melting into memory as
another stroke begins, the pattern repeating as long as I wish.

It is this I live for, that brief moment when we are bound
so tightly, where it is impossible to distinguish body from light
from water. A craving I can taste, a need that burns, a desire to
submerge myself in eternity.

I slice through the water, my hair billows around me like
Medusa's snakes. The warmth of a first kiss excites me, my skin
tingling in anticipation. My arms reach forward, my legs sepa-
rate, hoping, begging for touch. First, a fluttering on the back of
one leg, then the other, as tendrils slowly, excruciatingly wrap
around each limb. A whisper at the crux of my knee, a tickling

near my ankle, fingers tracing their way up the inside of each leg. Not in unison, one hand higher than the other, prolonging the sensation.

While fingers explore my skin, my neck feels first the coolness of the air, then warmth like waves breaking, pulling me back into their arms. My body comes alive, moisture flows from my sex, welcoming my lover. The light plays with me, teasing the insides of my thighs, exploring my skin, licking, tasting, kissing. I continue forward, binding myself tighter with each thrust. Sensation quickly runs down my back, hands firmly grasp my buttocks, pulling the cheeks apart as water flows through the crack, a tongue rimming my ass. I arch my back, trying to guide fingers toward my cunt that is aching with need. Soft laughter fills my ears as I realize I am too tightly bound to dictate touch or movement. I surrender, for the moment. As the last vestiges of control slip away I finally feel tongues and fingers envelop my pussy. I am in thrall to these wisps of light and the feel of water lapping at my very essence.

I respond to this panoply of lovers with every fiber of my being, relishing each taste, returning each touch, stroke for stroke. A cock enters me ever so slowly, my vagina expanding to accommodate the swelling. The geography of my inner walls kissing, sucking, fondling, marking its journey. My cunt muscles contract on withdrawal, memorizing shape and texture. The moment of loss that comes upon exit is balanced with the fullness of recurring penetration. The rocking motion of this exquisite fucking releases my clit from its hood. Tongues of light converge at its apex, lapping with great abandon.

My chest presses into the water, my nipples harden with passion. The water I displace surrounds me like a cocoon, soft, comforting. The air and light dance upon my body, faster and faster, their feet rippling with laughter, welcoming me. The intensity of it leading me to climax and a willingness to lock myself to only this, discarding all else.

With that comes panic. I lunge forward, breaking free, only to be bound again as the initial propulsion pales. My hands cup the water as one would a breast. My head breaks through the surface. With heaving breaths I gulp in air like a fish out of water. I descend again, then rise. I swim, breathing, denying breath, breathing, denying. The rhythm echoing in my ears, fear drumming into my soul.

I once saw, on television, whales mating. Moving effortlessly through water, side by side, the giant cock of one arcing across the other, following the curve of her body, covering nearly the circumference. They travel this way for days, fucking through hundreds of miles of water.

It is this scale of intimacy that drives me. To fuck like that, to savor, to explore, to taste and touch so completely, would bring us to orgasms of unfathomable intensity.

As I remember, my breathing steadies. My fears float away as if they had never bound me. I close my eyes, smiling as the light coils around me, holding me buoyant. My limbs reach out, gathering whispers of grace and beauty and love. I blanket myself within them. Once again I am caught in an intricate dance of light, water and life.

WHAT SHE HATH DESERVED

Alison Tyler

You have a twisted mind. You ought to be able to think of something suitable."

I was facedown on Dean's bed, and he was waiting, impatiently, for me to come up with my punishment, to name my poison. Just like in the Brothers Grimm's version of "The Goose Girl," in which an imposter princess is tricked into naming what ought to happen to someone who has behaved in the manner that she has. I knew better than to choose one of his regular toys of discipline because that would be too easy. A crop was fine for certain transgressions. But this was different. I'd asked his assistant, Marc, to lie to him. To lie for me. And Dean wouldn't tolerate such disobedience.

"You write all day," Dean said softly, bending now to be eye level with me.

That's true. But words come easier for me through my fingers than my lips.

"Untie me," I said, my voice raw.

Dean just stared.

"Untie me," I repeated. "Let me have my notebook."

His eyes narrowed. He didn't like this request, at all. Maybe because I didn't phrase the statement as a request.

"Please," I added. "Please, Dean. Let me get to my notebook. I'll write down what I think you should do to me...."

"What you think you deserve."

"Yes, Dean," I answered, more meekly. "Yes, Sir."

"A script?" he asked, and I knew he didn't want to act out something that I had penned, as if he were an actor, and I the director. No matter what we did, he needed to be in charge.

"No, Sir," I said quickly. "My penance."

Finally, Dean nodded. And smiled. He liked the concept, I could tell. He let me loose and then sat on the edge of the bed while I slid into panties, jeans, and a T-shirt. Casual, easy clothes for writing.

"You can't watch me work," I told him.

"You have a lot of demands." There was a warning in his tone.

"I won't be able to write if you're staring at me."

He stood up and looked at the clock on the nightstand. "You have an hour," he said. Like the witch in *The Wizard of Oz* with her nasty hourglass. Sixty minutes. I hadn't expected that.

Dean left the room, and I could hear the front door open and shut. He'd left the apartment, as well. I sat down on the bed with my notebook, and I stared at the blank page.

Blank. That was the perfect description of how I felt. I didn't have any idea what I should tell Dean to do to me. Finally, for inspiration, I opened the closet door and started to rifle through the contents. There was a variety of costume-style outfits: naughty nurse, prisoner of love, 1920s flapper girl. All sexy, sheer, short, and tight. And then I looked at the shelf at the top of the closet—the rows of boots, and high heels, and marabou-tipped slippers, and...

At the end of the row was a bag I hadn't noticed before. A doctor's bag. I stood on tiptoe to reach it. Dean had never pulled this out before, and it had been tucked in such a way that I had thought it was simply another one of my purses.

Inside the bag was a selection of realistic-looking medical devices. And suddenly I knew what to write about. I didn't know if I could handle what I was saying. Didn't know if Dean would even be into what I was writing. But the shame that filled me as I penned the words made me sure that I would at least get credit for effort. I wasn't going to stick to the same old style of punishment we'd played with in the past. Not a caning—public or private. Not a session in that hateful puppy cage. I spread out the various scary-looking items and started to write. The stainless steel speculums. The rectal thermometer. The rubber gloves, the old-fashioned enema syringe...

"She must be ill," Marc, the assistant, murmured to the doctor.

"Yes, definitely. If she were well, she'd never act in such a naughty fashion." A deep sigh. "We'll need to do a thorough exam to determine the cause. It would be against my judgment to punish her until we know the cause for her malfunction."

"What are you planning?" Marc asked, fingering the different items on the sterile tray.

"You'll take care of the preparations. The enema. The shower. Record her temperature in her chart. And then I want her spread out on the table and readied for me."

"Yes, Doctor."

My heart was pounding. I'd written stories that skirted this issue before, but never really delved into it. Naughty patient, strict doctor. That's nothing new. But the thought of Marc assisting Dean made me wet. And the knowledge that Dean had simply been waiting to play with me like this—that bag up there, where I could find it at any moment—that let me know that I must be on the right track. I crossed my legs tight and tried to continue. But in my head, I could already see Marc stripping me of my clothes, handing me some flimsy little hospital gown. Caring for me intimately at the instruction of his—and I had to say it, at least in my mind—Master. Because Marc was as much a slave as I was.

That thought stopped me. Just because I said the words, it didn't make them true. I had to consider the concept. But it rang right. Marc didn't simply punch a clock. No normal job re-quired an assistant to spank a boss's girlfriend. My head swam, and I tried my best to return to my story. One that I knew would be less fiction and more reality in a matter of minutes. Could I handle that?

I realized that there was no *me* in the piece. Not yet, any-way.

"Call her in."

The patient entered the room, head down, cheeks flushed pink.

"You know the rules," the doctor said, his voice stern, but calm. "Lying is a serious offence. But before you're properly caned, we'll need to make sure that you're fully capable of with-standing the punishment."

Oh, shit. Properly caned? Where the fuck had that come from? I crumpled the page and tossed it on the floor, then repacked the devices in that black medical bag and tucked it away once more at the top of the closet. I had to work to make the shelf appear undisturbed, and I was sheened with sweat by the time I sat down on the bed and started again.

What if I simply said that Marc should spank me for asking him to lie to Dean? He could bend me over one of the chairs in the living room. He could use his belt. That would make us even, wouldn't it?

I started to write once more. The clock was ticking. I'd wasted precious moments going through the closet for inspiration, wasted more time on that fucked-up Doctor fantasy. Now, I did my best to capture a scene Dean would appreciate. He'd never watched Marc spank me. He'd probably get a thrill out of that, right?

"Bend over the chair, Carla. Hold tight to the arms."

"Lift her skirt," Dean instructed. "And pull her knickers down."

"Of course—"

Marc's fingers gripped the waistband of Carla's lipstick-red panties and dragged them down her thighs.

"Step out of them, kid," Dean instructed. He was in charge. Even if Marc was doing the punishing. He was always in charge. "And hold still, doll. It's going to hurt. Right, Marc?"

"Yeah, Dean. That's the point isn't it?" A low laugh. "Why bother if it's not going to hurt?"

Carla lowered her head. She bit her bottom lip. She could hear Marc undoing the buckle on his belt, could hear the almost nonexistent sound of the leather being pulled free of the loops. In total silence, she waited for the first blow, wondering how many he would give her, how long she would manage to take the pain without crying—

The front door opened. I glanced at the clock. I was out of time. How the fuck had that happened? I swallowed hard, but kept on writing. Dean's footsteps coming down the hall spurred me on. I had nearly a full page of text by the time he pushed the door open. He took the notebook and read, his eyes following the text quickly. And then he handed the book back to me and picked up the crumpled piece of paper from the floor. As he spread the sheet out flat and began to read the discarded story, I saw a smile light his eyes, and I realized I was just like that idiot imposter princess in the fairy tale.

I'd named my punishment. Ordered my poison.

And now I would have to drink.

THE INTERIOR VIRGIN

L. A. Mistral

Look how her skin shines," said Julah. "It's like she's polished."

There was something about the Virgin. About the glow that seemed to emanate from her. About how its light seemed to draw them inside her bare shoulders and arms. This was a most uncommon portrait of the Virgin. Both Darin and Julah noticed it at once.

They leaned against each other on the long bench in one of the museum's many galleries. It was a slow day, and Darin and Julah could hear footsteps in corridors far away. They tilted their bodies toward one another's, as if the lead and gold of their bodies could tease the alchemy of insight from the painting directly in front of them.

The woman in the picture stood in a boat, her black hair flowing over the shoulders of her white gown. The boat was heading toward a body of land, seen over the Virgin's left shoulder. She stood facing the viewer, her mouth half open, as if she were about to tell a secret.

"Her skin's not being illuminated by anything," said Julah. "The light doesn't come from the outside in, but the inside out."

"Maybe it's the moon," said Darin. Darin was the older one. The one who always took things slower, more deliberately. She wore loose-fitting jeans and a button-down Oxford shirt. She was trying to be less buttoned-down. Julah, on the other hand, wore a tight, light sweater and low-cut corduroy jeans with a wide, thick belt. She was into high art and low explorations.

They stared a moment longer at the luminous skin of the woman in the painting and then Darin looked at Julah. She had noticed the same kind of light in Julah's skin the first time they met. At first she thought that it was Julah's translucent skin that seemed to shine. Darin was so curious that she wanted to kiss Julah's forehead and let her mouth travel slowly all the way down to the inside of her knees. But she didn't.

Even though this was only their second date, Darin couldn't help thinking about how Julah's thigh might taste. Again, Darin did not dare move.

"No, it's not the moon," Julah said, still looking at the painting.

There was something about the portrait of the Virgin that stirred Darin. The intense focus upon the Virgin's skin inspired Darin to listen to her own skin.

No one was around. Julah laid her head on Darin's shoulders and her brown hair dripped across Darin's neck. Darin shuddered.

"That's nice," Darin said close to Julah's ear. Her lips lingered for a moment just above Julah's earlobe, at the tender part. Then she nipped at it, her teeth teasing the lobe with the kind of bite you take when you eat new pears or salmon glazed with apricot.

Small bites, so that you don't spill any down your chin.

Darin eased closer to Julah and ran her fingernails across Julah's corduroy thigh. Julah felt her nipples harden. Darin brushed them with the tips of her fingers and pulled up her sweater. She bent down and licked Julah's skin across the belly. The sudden intimacy and coolness made Julah shudder again. In the shadow of the Virgin's portrait, something far from virginal was happening to her.

Darin turned quickly to the entrance. Two guards had poked their heads into the room. They just stared, watching the women sitting there close together, their thighs and shoulders touching. The guards, wearing dark blue uniforms, sized up the room. All the pictures seemed intact.

One guard said, "It's raining outside, now. Hope you have umbrellas."

Julah said, "We do, thanks," hoping they'd leave in a hurry. Then Julah lowered her voice and said, "It's getting wet in here too."

Darin muffled a laugh. The guards shrugged their shoulders and left, and Darin popped open the button on Julah's jeans. She slid Julah's zipper all the way down. Julah sighed like the sound of their hearts unzipping. Darin started to undo Julah's belt, then hesitated.

"What about the guards?"

"The spirit doesn't ask permission from the flesh," Julah said. "Besides, it's a wet Wednesday afternoon; the guards have a ton of gossiping to do."

Julah slid her pants over her hips and down past her knees. Darin noticed how Julah's legs seemed to glow, just like the Virgin's, and then she pressed her hand into the waist of Julah's panties. Julah took Darin's fingers and together they opened her pussy lips with ease.

Julah lay back and Darin reached into her pussy. Julah's cunt was as wide as a conch shell, and just as lovely. Her pussy smelled like sunlight and saltwater. Darin ground Julah's clit with the heel of her hand. Julah's hips rotated and she opened her legs wider to let Darin's fingers explore her more deeply. Darin slid two fingers, then three fingers inside Julah right up to the second knuckle. They stayed under like oyster divers, and they could hold their breaths for a long, long time.

"I fell in love with the Virgin when I was a kid in school. I loved her alabaster face and her flowing robes," Darin whispered. "I thought she was beautiful. The nuns caught me touching the statue, and forbade me to touch it ever again. Sometimes," she continued, "I have shy fingers."

"Not now you don't," Julah insisted. "Your fingers aren't shy."

"Disobedience is discovery," Darin said.

Julah turned slightly and undid the top three buttons of Darin's blouse. Darin wore a flesh-tone sling bra. Her bra barely contained her large, dark-nippled breasts. They didn't look as big beneath the formless Oxford shirt. It was easy for Julah to flip down one cup and ease Darin's large nipple into her mouth and suck it. It was large and erect with arousal. Darin felt a rush of desire pulse through her skin. Desire overcame fear and she slid two fingers out of Julah's cunt and plied them ferociously on Julah's clit. Julah leaned heavily against Darin, grinding her hips against Darin's thigh. Julah muffled her cries by biting into Darin's jacket.

Julah came hard, like a thoroughbred at the finish line. Her knees jackknifed and her back arched. She came in a skin-staggering swirl of scent and hushed sound.

Darin was breathing hard, too. She smelled the mixture of their sweat. *Aloe and ecstasy,* Darin thought. *Cinnamon and lotus stems.*

Darin ran her mouth across Julah's face. Julah had the same glow as the Virgin and the same glow as she had when they first met.

"It's the orgasm isn't it?" asked Darin. "That's what makes us glow."

Julah looked at the picture.

"The answer isn't in the picture. It's in us," Darin said. Her tongue and fingers listened for answers all that wet afternoon long. Now she knew. She continued to stir her fingers in Julah's sopping cunt, like she was a god mixing new galaxies.

She said, "Lust makes us light."

WHEN MY BOYFRIEND IS AWAY

Brooke Stern

Okay, so I always go a little crazy when my boyfriend goes away, but this time things are really bad. I worry about everything, and I'm a wreck waiting for him to get back. On the phone, he wants me to tell him everything, but I'm still afraid that if I talk about my doubts, they'll somehow come true. Why does the world seem to be so much scarier to me than to anyone else? I don't want him to hear my voice crack so I tell him I have to go, and get off the phone as fast as I can. That's what I do when I'm scared: I run away, abruptly and unceremoniously. It makes people think I'm mad at them when I'm only mad at myself.

After I hang up, I curl up under the covers and imagine poor Colin wondering why I blew him off. I'm sure I've made him feel awful, which only amplifies my anxieties. How do I get this out of control? I press my face into the pillow and feel a few tears wet the fabric. As if by instinct, I reach back and squeeze my fingers under the waistband of my skirt and panties. I touch my ass like a baby sucks her thumb, because it comforts me. I feel the faint tenderness from the spanking he gave me before he left and wish I could have another.

The urge always sneaks up on me and then refuses to leave, driving me to get my hairbrush from my dresser and pull my skirt and panties down around my thighs. I raise my arm high, grip the hairbrush hard, and promise myself to bring it down on my asscheek as hard as I can ten times no matter what. I make it to five and stop. Then I remember that I give up too easily, and I force myself to complete the promised ten strokes. I need to give myself the same on the other cheek, so I change hands, twist my body the other way, and do it again without much enthusiasm. My left hand is worse than my right, not because it hurts me more, but because it makes it even harder to give myself a proper spanking. I keep landing the hairbrush at weird angles and it feels more like bumping into the corner of the table with my hip than the stinging crack of a spanking. Besides, concentrating on my aim makes it impossible to let myself go. I throw the hairbrush on the floor and go back to crying into my pillow. Except I can't help it: as ridiculous as my attempt at self-discipline has been, I'm turned on. I want to push onward, but I can't think of what to do. Maybe I can humiliate myself.

Of course I can, I do it every day. This time it'll just be on purpose. I once read on a stupid website for dominants that a really good way to humiliate your submissive is to make her pee in her panties and wear the wet, cold panties afterward. The advice was just kinky enough to stay with me. I'm already walking down the hall to the bathroom when I realize I don't have to pee, at least not badly enough to wet my panties. I go to the kitchen and grab a couple of beers.

I drink the first beer quickly, sitting on the toilet with the lid down. I have my skirt pulled up around my waist and my panties around my ankles. I'm touching myself. When I'm done, I pull up my panties, step into the bathtub and spread my legs apart. The pee takes a minute to come. I'm strangely embarrassed by the delay, like I'm keeping someone waiting. Then it begins to soak my panties, wetting my whole pussy before it begins to leak out the sides and seep through the drenched fabric. The fabric becomes translucent, like a T-shirt in a wet T-shirt contest. It's unexpectedly awful to feel the warm wet spread through my panties and dribble down my legs.

I finish peeing and am hesitant to touch myself. I make myself do it with my panties on, so my fingers and my clit are grinding in pee. When I think about Colin watching me, I come hard. Then I look down and wonder what's become of me. Are other girls as weird as I am? Does anyone do the things that I do? I remember the first time I stuck my finger up my ass. For six months afterward, I saw reproachful looks and unsullied index fingers every time I looked at a woman and wondered if she'd ever done it. What woman pees her panties in her boyfriend's bathroom and enjoys it?

I take a shower and feel only a little cleaner afterward.

AS SHE WAS TOLD

Tenille Brown

Stephanie did as she was told. She lay there flat on her back, her eyes to the ceiling, knees up and thighs spread.

Her fingers…

Her fingers drummed on the dingy floral bedspread. Those very fingers were *supposed* to be resting on her cunt, preparing to find their way inside right about now, but she hadn't worked up to that yet.

It had been enough just to drive here, to rent a single room in the name of a Mrs. Jacqueline Jones, and then shed her clothes, all of them.

Her clothes…

They lay folded neatly on a chair in the corner of the room. Stephanie had found it strange that he'd even instructed her on what to wear when what he ultimately wanted was her naked. Still, he had insisted on a crisp yellow blouse and knee-length gray skirt. As for the shoes, he had demanded they be black, patent-leather heels.

And though one wouldn't peg Stephanie as the type to take orders, she did it all. She didn't question any of it, not the fact that he wanted the curtains to remain open or that he wished for the door to remain unlocked. She didn't even ask why he needed her to be lying on top of the covers, hiding nothing as people walked by.

Of course, she never questioned him. Questioning brought consequences, always. If she questioned or strayed from his specific instructions even slightly, he would resign himself to only talking to her about the weather, or he'd tell her about his dog's recent hip operation, or worse, he wouldn't talk to her at all.

So she learned to simply do as she was told.

With him, Stephanie always did as she was told.

And now, she stopped the nervous drumming and got to it. Slowly, her fingers crept over her hips and traveled down between her thighs.

Stephanie was wet.

She hadn't expected that. She had assumed she would be too aware of everything and every*one* around her to get turned on, but strangely, it fueled her, urged her to insert a finger, then two.

When she yearned for more, she reached for the box that lay on the floor beside the bed. He had mailed the package to her office and had included specific instructions on what to do with what was inside.

Stephanie had never used one before, didn't see how it could bring her any satisfaction. After all, this was a machine and she was a woman, a complicated woman.

Still, she twisted the base of the curved, leather cock until it began to swirl and vibrate in her hand. She moved it down between her thighs and slipped it inside.

And knowing that people could see her as they walked past, could hear her if their footsteps were soft enough, might enjoy her if they were bold enough to stop and watch, Stephanie trembled when she heard the click of heels on the concrete.

She halted, holding the machine deathly still between her legs, when a couple, who walked far apart from each other and kept their eyes to the ground, slowed, glanced briefly inside the window, then moved swiftly by.

Then Stephanie resumed, regaining her rhythm quickly.

So consumed was she with the pounding in her chest and the throbbing between her thighs, Stephanie didn't notice the maintenance man walk up and stop just outside the window. When she opened her eyes, he was propped against the railing, cigarette lit and dangling between his fingers.

She had been instructed on what to do if such an incident occurred, and so, as she was told, Stephanie continued. She inserted the stiff cock quickly, removed it slowly. She teased the edges of her cunt with the tip, arching her back and twisting on top of the covers.

The dark, wavy-haired man turned away when her eyes met his through the window, but, as if he couldn't help himself, he turned back again, his eyes fixated between her legs, his foot tapping nervously on the concrete.

When Stephanie looked more closely, she saw that between his long legs was an erection that pressed forward against his zipper. He crossed his legs just below the knee and leaned back, his elbows on the railing.

He took a final drag of his cigarette and put it out on the concrete. Then he brought his hand down to his crotch and unzipped his navy-blue trousers.

His cock sprang forward as if it had been waiting to be freed, waiting for just that moment when it could breathe. And just as suddenly, his hand was gripping the base, holding his thick, dark cock in place.

Stephanie spread her legs farther apart, excited by the thought of what could happen next, if the stranger so chose.

And he *did* choose.

One hand worked slowly on his stiff cock, the other he propped on the rail. Slowly, steadily he stroked, watching her. When the leather cock slipped deeper inside her, he licked his lips.

Stephanie's nipples hardened and rose like pearls on her breasts. The one thing she *hadn't* been told was that she'd enjoy it, even hunger for more. She wondered if she were stepping out of line, if she'd somehow be reprimanded for her own pleasure.

And he would know that she had enjoyed it just a little more than she should. He always knew.

The thought caused Stephanie to hesitate. Then, just as suddenly as he had begun, the man outside her window stopped stroking, tucked his still rigid cock back into his pants and stepped out of sight.

She paused. Had he seen someone coming? Was he suddenly afraid? Embarrassed?

When Stephanie realized that he had never passed the second window, that he had halted just outside her door, she pondered: Would he take it upon himself to push the door open and come in? Had he merely stepped closer so that he could hear her?

And as if he *was* listening, as if his ear *was* pressed against the door, Stephanie resumed, her moans growing louder, her thrusts more intense. The dildo circled and shook insider her.

And then, on top of the tasteless, dingy bedspread; flat on her back, knees up, thighs spread wide, Stephanie came.

She allowed herself to catch her breath only for a moment before she stood on her feet, cunt wet with desire, skin glistening with sweat.

Stephanie stepped back into her clothes, not even looking toward the bathroom or the sink. And as she had been told to, she placed the used dildo back in its box and tucked it under her arm.

She paused at the door, listening for signs that the stranger was still there, and hearing nothing, she opened the door and walked out.

She looked down and smiled; stepped over the thick, wet result of the stranger's passion; and, as she had been told to, stuffed the box inside her shoulder bag and walked quietly away.

THE PERFECT SEASON

Rachel Kramer Bussel

For some people, the crackling hot sun of summer is torturous; they can live with the refreshing warmth of June and July, but come August they tend to hibernate in front of their air conditioners. But me? Well, summer is my favorite season, for many reasons, and right up there is that I love the taste of my husband Steve's sweat. Ever since I took my first lick of his neck, way back when we were in college, I've lusted after him. In fact, I licked his neck before I even kissed him, needing to know how his skin, his very essence, tasted. He was salty and tangy, and there was a faint hint of cologne mixed in there. I proceeded to tongue my way all around his neck before I moved upward to nibble his earlobe and finally, after I'd felt around and found his cock achingly hard, let our lips melt together.

Ever since then, for the last decade, I've lusted after his sweat. In the summertime, all we really have to do is walk outside and we both start to melt; well, I do in more ways than one. Yesterday was a pretty average day; wiped out from the workweek (I'm a lawyer and he's a banker), we decided to stay in, watch some movies and cook a meal together. Problem was, our fridge was beyond empty, so we had to leave the lovely air-conditioning to get the ingredients. Even though we live in New York and shop right around the corner, the sun was so strong that by the time we got up the two flights of stairs, we were both hot. We plunked down the groceries and then, as I went to put the mint-chocolate-chip ice cream into the freezer, I felt him come up behind me. "Baby, what is it about your ass that just makes me want to devour you?"

He put his arms around me, nudging his cock against my butt while I stood with the freezer door open, the frozen pint in my hand as the chilly air wafted against my heated cheeks. Down below, my other set of cheeks was being squeezed and fondled by Steve, and when he peeled down my short shorts, I didn't resist. I knew I was wasting energy by leaving the freezer open, but somehow when Steve sank to his knees, I didn't care all that much about the environmental effects of my actions. He fondled my asscheeks, squeezing them in just the way he knows will make my pussy tingle, while tugging my thong upward so the fabric bisected my pussy lips and made my clit throb with need.

Everything Steve was doing to me felt so good—and with the cold air blowing on my face while his tongue began to slide against that slim line of flesh where my cheeks met, wetting the thin strip of my thong—I almost forgot about my sweat lust as I pushed my ass backward toward him, my pussy getting juicier by the minute. I could practically feel my lower lips swell in arousal. When he stopped licking me and instead stood up, pushed his fingers under my panties and into my dripping slit, and leaned forward, resting his sweaty brow against the bare skin of my back above the low line of my tank top so I felt the wetness rub against my own damp skin, I went wild. I clamped down around his fingers, urging him deeper, while he rubbed his face against my back and then moved higher to lick the back of my neck and sink his teeth into the tender skin.

I moaned and turned around to face my sexy husband, who still gets me off just as much as he did when we were younger and freer. We fucked every day back then, and now, amazingly, despite all our adult responsibilities, we still managed to maintain a steady diet of all kinds of sex, enough to keep me always teetering on the edge of arousal, coming down from a climax or preparing for one. As I kissed his lips frantically and then turned my head to his sweaty neck, I feasted on my favorite summer sweet treat—him.

I worked my way down from his neck to his beaded nipples. I leaned down, my ass brushing against the cool refrigerator door as I worked each tiny nub into an even harder, higher peak. Steve moaned, "Oh, Tara, yes," and some other unintelligible sounds as I proudly ignored his cock and went about slapping my tongue against his nipples, then gently biting the puckered flesh surrounding them, until finally his fingers came down onto my head, threading through my long, black hair as he shuddered. I stilled, breathing against his little nubs, still amazed that I could provoke such a powerful reaction from such minuscule pieces of flesh. The magic of the human body, or rather, Steve's very specific human, male body, never ceases to thrill me.

After I'd licked to my tongue's content, I moved downward, inhaling his manly musk with each movement. My heels were touching each other and so close to my pussy, and when heels and pussy met, I started to slide. I steadied myself against his strong hands and continued my mouth's journey. He knew that he had to sit still if he was going to get what he—and I—most wanted. Licking his stomach, that soft gentle bit of skin set against so much sturdy muscle, hovering so close to his pole, is one of my favorite moments. I teased him by lingering there even while his cock bobbed so near me, licking up every drop of sweat I could find, then kissing my way downward until I got to his wiry pubic hair and kissed that too.

When I assault Steve with my tongue, I want him to know how much I treasure him, how much my body craves his, needs him, wants what he has to offer. Only when I've made that perfectly clear do I take that next step and let the head of his dick part my eager lips. I subtly slipped my fingers down between my lips and stroked myself slowly, sensually, as if the two parts of me were merging into one seamless machine as I continued to swallow him. I moved slowly, slyly, but I was no match for the force of our combined arousal, and soon his come was streaming into my mouth, while my own juices dribbled onto my fingers. I let my whole body go, my throat going slack as he gave me what I wanted most.

When I'd swallowed every last drop and wrung as much pleasure from my pussy as I could stand, I stood, rubbing my wet body up against his. "Let's take a shower," I said, "and then make ourselves sweaty all over again." He swooped me up in his arms and carried me to the bathroom.

Summer really is the perfect season, giving us plenty of ways to cool off, and even more ways to heat up.

MUFF DIVER

Shanna Germain

I have a thing for guys who won't go down. Unlike most girls I know, I prefer a guy who simply doesn't bother with the whole mess. Wham-bam-thank-you-ma'am with a little kissing thrown in for good measure, that's much more my preference. Who needs some guy down on his belly, crawling up your crotch, playing tongue-whistle on your most sensitive organs? Not me, that's for sure.

I mean, it sounds nice, but there are so many reasons not to, they far outweigh any reason to do it.

First of all, there's the whole reciprocal thing, which means that every second a guy's got his face buried between my thighs, I feel like we're punching a fair-trade time clock. Three minutes of him eating me out means I have to spend at least that much time down on my knees running my tongue along the shaft of his cock and murmuring about how much I like sucking him off. And let me tell you, it's hard to count the seconds off when you've got your mouth wrapped around a guy's pipe and he's moaning so loud you can't hear yourself think.

And then there's the skill thing: half the time, when some guy's got his head buried down between my legs, he's either jamming his tongue into my holes or he's licking my clit like it's an envelope that won't seal tight. First, though, he gets down there and starts snuffling and nuzzling through my hairs like he's a dog hoping to find something good buried beneath those brown curls. Then he starts licking tentatively, trying to burrow his tongue down into the wrong spot, then backing up and starting over, like he can't tell where one lip begins and the other ends. So he'll start licking the insides of my thighs, supposedly to get me hotter, but really because he's trying to orient himself to my anatomy. Then he's back at me with his hot tongue, trying to find the open sesame that's going to let him inside my golden gate.

Sometimes a guy makes it—the right pressure or angle can go a long way—but most of the time it goes on so long I have to reach down and help him, open myself to him so he doesn't feel so bad for doing all that work and not getting any response. But as soon as I do that—hold myself open with my fingers spread wide—he narrows in on my clit like a hunting dog, yelping and poking it with his tongue. Before I know it, he's sucking on my clit as if it's a drop of dew and he's a parched man crawling through the desert. Lick, lick, slurp, it's more than I can handle, knowing I'm getting his face all wet with my juices, sometimes to the point where he has to wipe his chin off on a corner of the sheet. He starts poking my clit with his tongue as if it's a tooth he wants to knock loose, and all of a sudden, the dumb thing is swelling and swelling, making an even bigger target for him to poke at.

And the whole time, the rest of my naked body's just getting left out in the cold, and my poor aching nipples are crying for attention, and here all this guy's interested in is getting my clit between his teeth. Occasionally, he'll reach out and give my thigh a slap or tweak my nipples a little, but really, it gets so lonesome up here sometimes that I have to give my tits some attention of their own. I give them a gentle tweak or two, talking to them all the while so they don't feel lonely. "Oh, yeah, you like that, don't you girls?"

Of course, all that attention I'm giving my own body is making me hot and wet, and now he's got his whole face buried in me so far I'm wondering how he can breathe. But I figure it's his problem—he'll figure it out eventually. And usually, he comes up for air right about the time that he decides he wants to stick something beside his tongue into one of my holes. He starts burrowing one finger into my twat, and has another one running around and around the outside of my asshole, and I can tell he's getting ready to take the plunge. He keeps licking and licking, his tongue going up and down like it's attached to a nine-volt battery, and wiggling one finger inside me until I'm about ready to tell him to quit it already, I hate this stuff anyway.

And then the waves start rippling through me and I'm shuddering and shaking and moaning like a little baby. And the whole time, the guy's looking up from between my legs like he's the king of the world, fingers still in me, wet chin and all.

And I hate that, I tell you. I hate it.

WATER LOVE

J. Sinclaire

There was no special occasion to prompt our trip to the honeymoon capital of the world. No anniversary celebration or birthday present. We certainly weren't eloping. So what was our motivation to suddenly take off in the middle of a workweek to a lavish hotel three hours away?

Simply put: fucking.

Or even more simply, we needed to cross off *sex in a Jacuzzi* from our sexual adventures list. So when I found a supercheap hotel package that included a king-size bed, natural gas fireplace, full shower and two-person Jacuzzi, I did what any sane person would. I told my boss I needed to take a few days off due to a family emergency. He was very understanding.

I gave Curtis the good news when he got home.

"You're going to be sick today and tomorrow."

He eyed me curiously until I explained about the hotel and Jacuzzi. And that is how we arrived at the hotel with the huge freaking Jacuzzi in the middle of the room.

We threw our bags in the corner and inspected what would be our new home for the next forty-eight hours. The bed was very soft, with fresh new sheets we would certainly soil in no time. The shower could fit us both comfortably as well and the placement of the mirrors in the washroom was definitely handy. Put it all together and we had the makings of an indoor vacation for two.

I walked him over beside the tub and wrapped my arms around his neck, looking into his green eyes.

"Well? Where should we start?"

He pretended to be lost in thought as he slipped his hands under my shirt and slowly began to undo my bra. He made quick work of it and moved his hands to my front to claim his prize.

"This seems like a good place to get things going," he said as he pinched one of my nipples, then drew the fabric of my shirt and bra up and over my head. He lowered his mouth to tease my nipples with his tongue, pulling on them occasionally with his teeth. His hands were on my hips, keeping me in place though it was highly unlikely I would be running off anywhere.

Dropping to his knees, he kissed a trail down to my belly button, pausing at the clasp on my jeans. His hands moved down the outside of my legs before sliding up along my inner thighs, rubbing smoothly over my crotch as he began undoing my pants. He groaned his approval when he found that I had conveniently not worn panties. I stepped out of my pants just in time for his lips to seek out mine, parting them with his tongue as he searched for the hard nub of my clit. He guided me backward so that I was sitting on the edge of the Jacuzzi, spread open for him.

Barely lifting his head, he mumbled, "Turn on the water." I tried to comply with his request as best I could, considering the pressure of his tongue on my clit was already making my hands unsteady. Somehow, I got the water running at a comfortable temperature and the Jacuzzi began to fill up.

His hands were on my thighs, keeping my legs parted as he lapped at my lips. He was such a tease. He would go from light flicks of his tongue over my lips to deep heavy licks that delved inside me. Within minutes I was writhing in pleasure.

"I think it's time to get wet."

I laughed before kissing him deeply. "Oh honey, I'm way ahead of you there."

He stood up, taking his shirt off quickly. I undid his pants, his cock springing free and at attention. I licked the tip of it before turning away to mind the tub. The Jacuzzi was almost full so I turned the water off, switched the jets on and got in. I beckoned him to join me, sliding my hand around his dick and guiding him into the tub. He went to sit down beside me but I positioned myself quickly in front of him and began teasing his head with my tongue. I licked the length of his shaft as my hands caressed his balls. I heard him sigh as I took him into my mouth, fitting as much of his long hard length inside me as possible. I wanted to tease him for hours but my pussy wanted him inside me more. I sucked him roughly, plunging him inside my mouth with a fast steady rhythm before pulling him away and guiding him down into the water with me.

He sat down against one corner of the Jacuzzi, the jets swirling water around us and making it hard to see what was happening underneath. The water was high, touching the bottom of my tits as I straddled him. It was such a rush to not actually be able to see his cock but suddenly feel it straining at the entrance to my pussy. He pulled me to him, sucking on my nipples like a starved man as his hands guided me down onto him. I moaned as he slid inside me, inch by exquisite inch, until I had encompassed him completely. The water swirled over my sensitive nipples, making me gasp at the power of the jets.

He took my lower lip in his mouth, nipping at it as I started to move on him—slowly, oh so slowly at first, letting him slip almost all the way out of me before plunging back down on him. We began to realize that our actions were sending water sloshing all over the place but we hardly cared at that moment. I picked up the pace, guided by his hands on my hips, and I could feel my orgasm beginning to build inside me. I kissed him frantically, urging him on as he began to buck his hips, hitting my G-spot at the perfect angle. He slid a hand between us to rub my clit and suddenly I was coming, clenching myself around him. The heat and motion of the water added to my climax as my whole body felt caressed by him. He shuddered at the tightening of my pussy and let himself go a minute later, spurting inside me as he groaned and buried his face in my neck.

We sat there, just trying to focus on breathing as the sensations melted away. I eventually looked around to see that we had managed to get quite a lot of water onto the hotel room carpet.

"Oops."

He noticed it as well and began to chuckle, his softening cock still inside me. It sent us both into fits of laughter and even a week later, when we got the $126 cleaning bill for the carpet, we couldn't help but giggle.

Money well spent to cross that off the list!

FLYING

Sasha White

M y stomach jumps with excitement and I shift my weight
from one foot to the other. I look around at the people
surrounding me and wonder what their reactions would be if
they could read my mind. Their tense faces and rumblings to
each other tell me they're not happy about the long line.

I shift my weight again, enjoying the friction between my
thighs as I do it. I bring my legs tighter together and the seam
of my pants digs in a little more. Shifting my weight continu-
ally from one foot to the other, I concentrate on the arrows of
pleasure my movements cause. I tighten my inner muscles and
relax them once. Then again.

My heart is pounding and my nipples harden, aching for attention. Someone leaves the line and steps up to the counter and
everyone shuffles forward, shifting luggage as they go. I make
a show of shifting my backpack and tightening the strap across
my chest, then resume my rocking from side to side, as if I were
in a trance. But now, the tightened strap is rubbing back and

forth across my nipples with every shift of my weight.

I can't help myself. I begin to clench and unclench my inner muscles rhythmically. The pack strap is rubbing on my hard nipples; the seam of my pants is now directly stimulating my clit and shooting shafts of pleasure into my core. I close my eyes and let the climax come. My breath hitches in my throat and a small but powerful orgasm rumbles through my body.

When I open my eyes, the line's shifted forward again, and I'm next. My heart pounds and anticipation flows hotly through my veins. The woman behind the counter waves me forward and asks for my papers.

Familiar with the routine, I heft my backpack off and lift it onto the scale, doing buckles up and tucking in straps so they won't get caught on anything.

After a moment of typing at her computer she hands me back my papers and points me in the right direction. "Your flight starts boarding at three o'clock, gate fourteen. You need to clear security first. There are shops and restaurants after you pass through, so you can do so at any time now. Enjoy your flight, Miss Anderson."

I head off with a grin on my face. Traveling has always made me feel daring, and free. Judging by my excitement at just being in line at the check-in desk, this time was no different. My plan is to enjoy the flight, the holiday, and whatever else comes my way.

A familiar tingle runs through my body as I wait, once again in line, for my chance to pass through the security checkpoint. On the other side of the metal detectors and scanners I can see people rushing from one gate to another, others relaxing in the seats waiting for their flights to be called. I also see shops full of knickknacks, candy and magazines. Then I notice a good-looking man flipping through a magazine in the nearest one, and heat pools low in my belly.

Yes, I do plan on enjoying my flight. And everything else that comes my way.

THE COVERS OF BOOKS

Marie Potoczny

Mark was nursing a coffee—black—when I sidled up next to him, and took out my favorite copy of *Pride and Prejudice* to pass the time until my best friend failed to materialize.

He smiled crookedly, Mark did, and asked, nodding toward my book, "Are they making that into a movie?"

His cockiness made my pussy gush like the Hoover Dam had just collapsed.

"I didn't think anyone read Austen," he said, grinning, "unless they were making it into a movie."

"It's a classic." I was offended at the accusation that I was a trendy reader and clutched the book to my heart.

"Sorry. No offense." He reached out and touched my knee in atonement. "May I?" He pried the book from my hands to quote passages. I was hooked like the first line of an Austen omnibus.

After a few java cocktails, we played the who's who of authors, trying to out-impress each other by naming the most difficult and obscure writers in some sort of sick, quasi-intellectual flirting ritual.

He said he adored Jane Austen and Elizabeth Bennet was his favorite heroine; this was a better character recommendation than if he had been introduced by my grandmother.

"Me, too!" I squealed.

"Really?" He studied my face. "Come to think of it, you do look like Ms. Bennet."

"I've been told that before," I lied.

Mark struggled to say something, seemed at a loss for words, stammered, and then grabbed my hands in that awkwardly sincere way I imagined Mr. Darcy would have with Elizabeth at the conclusion of the novel.

His eyes searched mine. He petted my hand, the pads of his fingers grazing the insides of my wrists, our digits becoming tangled in the fervor and mounting necessity to fuck.

I took him home. Mark hitched his penis to my carriage, and we laughed while he screwed me, up and down, over and over. Apparently he preferred the abridged version; from coffee shop to finish it took less than an hour.

He lingered for a couple of minutes, thumbed through my Penguin classics, and smirked at a comment I'd written in the margin of *Emma*, before he tugged on his pants and headed out.

"Where are you going?" I asked, as the door closed behind him.

I returned to the coffee bar the next night to find Mark. He was there, but a brunette with a plain face now occupied the table beside him.

She was reading a copy of *Jane Eyre*.

A RIVER WITH TWO MOUTHS

Stephen D. Rogers

Until you've tasted your pussy on another woman's lips, you haven't lived. I have, thanks to a boyfriend who knows he has nothing to fear.

In fact, I was the one who was nervous about putting the idea into action. That's why Brad didn't give me a choice.

How it happened was this: We'd been experimenting with light bondage. Brad would tie me up or blindfold me. Sometimes both. One time, cotton ropes wrapped my wrists and ankles, a silk scarf covered my eyes; Brad kissed me harder than usual. I arched up off the bed trying to swallow his mouth.

He broke away. "I love you."

"I love you." I could feel his hot breath on my cheek.

And then I could feel a different breath on the sole of my foot.

There was no way Brad could have moved that quickly, not when I could still feel his lips on my ear.

His voice became a whisper. "Her name is Lori."

The breath on my foot became a tongue. The tongue became a warm river winding through my toes, a river that flowed over my foot, danced around my ankle, and raced up the inside of my leg until it reached the source.

I felt her on me, in me, and I would have melted away if the cotton ropes had not kept me in place, such were the sensations caused by her wet tongue.

Brad continued to whisper in my ear, a warm murmur of sounds more arousing than mere words.

And then the dam burst and I overflowed, myself a raging river.

I caught my breath just in time for her lips to cover mine, hers moist with my own fragrant juice. She kissed me and then she was gone, without a word, without my getting so much as a single glance at the face that had brought me so much pleasure.

MARKS, REVIEWED

Debra Hyde

These marks I bear speak volumes. They say that I gave myself to you, without reserve, wholly, completely. They claim that you took what I offered and used me as you saw fit. I was your canvas, tightly wound rope was your medium, and now my hands and feet are as striped as a tabby's coat. And catlike, I rub them against each other to feel the sweet burn of these bruises. Luscious is their tenderness.

Fresh out of bondage, my breasts sport marks, too. Rings of red encircle them, like ripples on water. I cup my breasts, press them together and sigh, then rub my nipples lightly. They're tender from the clamps you used on me. Ah, those clamps! They bit into me, into flesh made soft by the hold of bondage. The pain seared but in bliss and surrender, just the way I like it.

Like an afterthought, my poor nipples remind me of our times together. I recall you putting clamps to them, making me don a blouse, then taking me to a bookstore. Our browsing probably looked aimless, but still I wonder if anyone spied us when you reached in between my buttons, found the chain and pulled me into pain. I had to stifle my cries that night, stuffing them down into a silence I didn't know I had.

I give myself to you because I love you and I love what you do to me. Because you deftly control the action we share. Because you test me as you control me. You use me to create our erotic edge.

A hand joins mine on my breast. I look up to find you settling onto our bed, smiling. "You look good," you tell me, admiring the marks you've given me. "So good."

Your admiration has a lusty tone as you kiss me and take me by the wrists. You're holding the rope again. I can't see it as I kiss you with closed eyes, but I feel the weight as you capture my wrists. Roughly, the rope caresses the existing marks and they protest the pain.

You push me down on the bed and draw my bound hands up above my head. You stretch the ropes tightly, tying them to the rails of my old brass bed. My old bed, the one item that has followed me from the innocence of childhood to the trials of adulthood, trials that achieve new twists each time you take me. This bed, which long ago shielded me from the monsters of the dark, now hosts the monsters of our desires. My nighttime sanctuary is your anytime playground.

More rope encircles my ankles. You draw my legs up and tie the rope to the metal rungs of the footboard. It spreads me wide, lifts my ass from the bed, and exposes the pit of my pleasure. I am accessible.

But my legs strain. This isn't an easy position and I wonder how long I'll be able to maintain it.

You bring your lips to my sore nipple and murmur "This won't take long," as you nibble there. I moan as your teeth clasp me lightly, as your tongue flicks across my hard ruby of a nipple.

You rise from my breast and, positioning yourself, hover over me. Your stiff, ready cock seeks out its target, encouraging my nether lips to open. When they do, my damp eagerness beckons to you. You breech me, enter me, take me. You feel massive.

My legs tremble, strained and compromised. If they were free, I'd wrap them tight around your waist and never let go. But I cannot offer myself up to you that way. Instead, I remain passive as you initiate your final act in this drama we share.

There's something sweet in that surrender, in giving myself to you to use and enjoy. Swift, steady strokes overtake me. You pant in my ear, sounding like a wild, rutting animal. You ram me, and it feels delicious. My cunt grows tight around you as you work me. It aches to be torn asunder, it begs you to greater cruelties, and suddenly a rich spasm of orgasm overwhelms me.

I'm still breathless when you nuzzle into my neck, nip me, then bear down. I stiffen and cry out, orgasm forgotten. Long, deep stabbing strokes accompany your bite. You're so ferocious that I weaken. My legs are like putty and my cunt goes numb.

Your teeth go deeper. I tense and scream. I want to thrash about but I can't, I'm bound, I'm helpless. You absorb the agony of my desire and it heightens you, bringing you ever closer. Your body begins to quiver, preparing for that which is about to peak, and I know you're there when you gasp for breath and slam deeply into me. Your proof invades me, warm and wet.

We collapse then, you upon my body, me still caught in your web, and as we do, the bed moans. It echoes our drama, becoming the coda to our lust. As we rest, I realize that my bed, this sanctuary of mine, sighs sweetly for us, and I sigh in kind for all we have and all we share.

TASTING KATE

Jolie du Pré

Kate had moved to Manhattan and kept writing even when I ignored her letters. I'd grown to hate her when she lived in Chicago, but she didn't know that. She was one of the most beautiful girls in college, and I was just another one of her many friends, following her around like a starstruck fan. She had no idea I was in the closet wishing I could fuck her brains out.

My therapist is probably still shaking. For the past couple of months she's been trying to get me to commit to something, to go for something; to help me figure out why, after college, all I've wanted to do is wait tables at a crappy restaurant, why I panic every time I look at a blank canvas even though I have an art degree, why I can't seem to sleep through the night.

"If you had one wish, what would it be?" she'd asked me.

"Why do you want to know?" I responded.

"Because then maybe we can help you get it."

We looked at each other in silence until a smile crept upon my face.

"You look like you have something!" she exclaimed, clutching her hands together like a proud parent.

"Yeah, I do. If I had one wish, I'd taste Kate."

"What do you mean?"

"I mean, I want to taste my friend. Only I can't, because she's all the way in New York and anyway, she's straight."

"Oh...oh...you mean..." That's when her hands started to shake. Poor thing.

"Yeah, that's what I mean. So you got any big ideas as to how I can do that?" She looked at the floor, trying to think of what to say. It was priceless. You shouldn't ask a question if you're not prepared to hear the answer.

"Deanna," she said, looking at me again. "You could be doing so much more with your life."

Blah, blah, blah. She went on like that for about five minutes until my session was up.

Now I'm sitting on a plane, headed for New York to see the woman I hate. She melted me, that tease; her pleas for a visit won out.

I arrive at LaGuardia. So many different people thrown together like a tossed salad. And there stands Kate.

"Hey, you! Welcome to New York."

She hasn't changed. Her blonde hair is still long and silky. She still wears peasant skirts. And she still doesn't wear a bra. I want to grab those perfect globes every time I see them. Hippy cunt. It used to draw me in, all that love and energy emanating from that gorgeous body, but now I just wish she would stand back.

Instead, she gives me a hug. Her neck smells like fresh lemons, and I fight the urge to kiss it. I pull away, but I'm polite. "Kate, you look great as always. Let's get to your place. I'm sick of airports."

"Yes, you must be starved, too. I'll make you some curried tofu."

Kate always used to push her health food on me. I enjoyed it at the time, eating something she made. But now I have visions of chowing down on a burger, just to piss her off.

We take a cab to her apartment, this little thing fifteen floors up.

"We've got this place to ourselves this weekend," Kate says. "Lori's gone to Ohio to visit her parents."

I peek into Lori's room. What a pig! I thought I was bad.

"Don't look in there. There's probably food or maybe even some dead humans rotting under all that junk," Kate says.

"Where should I sleep? On the couch?"

"You're kidding, right? You'll be bunched up like a sardine. No, you'll sleep with me."

I'd slept with Kate before, just like two little girlfriends. It was torture, especially when her body would roll against mine.

"Of course, there's always Lori's bed, if you can find it," Kate smirks.

"No way! Your bed sounds fine," I say.

"Good, now let's get some lunch into you."

At night, we go to a club and dance. Rather, Kate does. I just watch her. She sashays across the floor, swinging her hips and bouncing those breasts. I watch the guys line up and I'm mesmerized. She does this to me every time.

We go home, and while Kate drinks some concoction to cleanse her system, I go into the bathroom and put on my nightgown. Even though I usually can't sleep through the night, I'm determined to try.

I step out of the bathroom and then I can't move.

"I sleep in the nude, Deanna. Have for a while now."

Fucking bitch sends my cunt into a tailspin. I've never seen nipples so large and pink, right there in front of me. And just a little patch of hair on her pubes. This must be penance for all the evil I've done. I should have stayed in Chicago. I never should have replied to that letter.

We climb into bed and I stare up at the ceiling. She turns off the light by the side of the bed, and I am acutely aware of her breathing and the smell of her skin. Her flesh is hot and I know it, even though I haven't touched her.

She turns her head. It's dark, but I know she's looking at me. I know this woman with those juicy tits is staring at me.

If you had one wish, what would it be?

I take my hand and place it gently on her thigh. My heart is beating like crazy.

But then Kate grabs my hand, brings it to her pussy and plunges my fingers into her. God, she's so wet.

My fingers are still inside her when she climbs on top of me and plops her breast in my mouth. I suck so hard on that nipple it sticks straight out. I do the same to the other one, and we're moaning so loud I'm sure the neighbors can hear.

And then she kisses me. Such soft lips. My head is spinning. Her mouth leaves mine and I hear her scream, "Oh god, Deanna!" She comes like a fountain on my hand.

When she rolls off me, my fingers fall out of her slippery cunt and go directly into my mouth. I coat my lips with her juices and take in her sweet smell. I'm tasting Kate.

As she cuddles against my side, we fall asleep.

And for the first time in a long while, I don't wake up until morning.

RUN-IN

Tsaurah Litzky

My ex-husband grew up on a farm. Once he bragged to me he learned to do it by watching the animals. When the hog mounted the sow, he said, the hog was an unstoppable force. "But I'm not a pig," I protested. "Yes, you are," he told me. "You're a pig for me." It was true. All day when he was at work, I hungered for his cock; at night I feasted on it. With my mouth I sucked and nibbled it, with my cunt I swallowed it up again and again. After we split, I did not want his cock meat or any other part of him; or so I told myself. Still, five years later, I often find myself dreaming that he is moving inside me, and in the morning I wake with my hands between my legs.

When I ran into him last Friday on Broadway in front of Dean & DeLuca, he didn't look like a farm boy. I hadn't seen him since he moved back to Canada. He was wearing a black leather jacket that had to be expensive and black velvet slacks. I wondered if he was dealing drugs again, but I wasn't going to ask.

His first question to me was, "Are you still with Paul?" I

told him, "Of course," lying like Pinocchio, and then I quickly changed the subject.

"What brings you down here?" I asked.

"I have a show coming up at Castelli's."

I wondered if he was making the show up to impress me, but I didn't ask him the dates or any of the particulars. I was distracted because my nipples had suddenly hardened into sharp little spikes. He still had that effect on me.

"You and Paul happy?" he asked.

"Ecstatic," I answered. I didn't tell him how I had taught Paul to replicate all his farm-boy moves. Then my ex went on, "I heard your novel was published. Am I in it?"

"Absolutely not. It's a fantasy, a total fantasy." The truth was he was on every page.

"Listen," he said, "if you're not in a hurry, let's have a drink, for old times' sake. We could go to Dante's. Is Larry still working there?"

"Why should I have a drink with you?" was my reply. "And Larry's been gone for ages." I started to walk away. He came after me. "Come on, what are you frightened of?" he asked. I was walking a shaky tightrope suspended over a bottomless pit. I fell.

"Okay," I said.

Dante's was packed, four deep at the bar. Many of the patrons were already looped, talking loudly, wild eyed. "The Evil Empire is upon us," bellowed an old gent with bushy gray hair. "Yeah, sure, sure, but now it's hopeless," cried his friend, a bald fat guy wearing dark glasses. "Luke Skywalker is dead, he died trying to stop the plane from hitting the second tower."

The old gent pushed his face right into his friend's. "It's your fault, all you do is read Robert A. Heinlein books, you didn't even vote, now we got a fascist country."

His friend shot back, "It's always been a fascist country, that's why I read sci-fi."

The young guy next to him standing with his pretty redheaded girlfriend cut in, "Your generation blew it, next the maniac in the White House will outlaw thinking." They both turned on him. "Who asked you?" yelled the old guy. "Shove it in your ear," hissed his friend.

The kid snapped back at him. "Gonna make me?" he said, raising his arm, his hand curled into a fist. His girlfriend pulled his arm down. "Cut it out, Roger," she said. "Don't go there. You know perfectly well since nine eleven, we're all nuts."

"You're so right," said the bartender, intervening. "Let me buy drinks all around."

"You yanks are still fucked up," said my ex.

"More then ever," I told him.

We pushed our way to the back of the room to stand by the long counter opposite the bathroom. He went back to the bar, scored us drinks and brought then back.

"To old times," he said.

"I don't want to drink to that," I told him. We stood silently facing each other, our eyes locked. The crowd pressed in on us, forcing me so close to him our bodies were touching. His jacket was open and my tits brushed against his chest. My nipples were still hard, so hard I wondered if he could feel them through the fabric of his shirt. My body always speaks true at the same time that it betrays me.

We drank our beers, still looking at each other. A big brunette came out of the bathroom, wearing a low-cut scoop-neck sweater. The tops of her fleshy white knockers were visible down to the rosy nipple. He did not even glance at her tits; he was looking so intently at me, his mouth open slightly. I could see his thick pink tongue glistening, the tongue that had licked my every inch, even between my toes, even my little back hole.

I could not resist the dark force of desire growing within me. I reached my hand out, grabbed the waistband of his pants and just pulled him along behind me for the few steps right into the bathroom. I turned and locked the door. The small bathroom was designed for one person at a time with only a commode and a sink. I stood in front of the sink, took off my coat and dropped it on the floor. I bent over, hiked my skirt up in the back. It was he who pulled my tights and panties down to my knees.

"Bend over more," he said. I grabbed the sink for balance and shut my eyes. I heard the sound of a zipper opening, then his hands were on my ass, cradling, stroking, showing me he remembered how ass play always drove me wild. Then one hand moved down and around, until his fingers found my clit and circled it, milking it. His other hand went to my nether lips, pulling them wide. I curled my hips up, offering my ready cunt. And then he was inside; it was the perfect fit, like always the hog and the pig.

Like the little oinker I am, I started to squeal and came immediately.

"Can I let go inside you?" he asked. "I don't have a condom." Neither did I. I felt like just saying "Go ahead," so much did I want his white fire inside me, but then he said, "No, I better pull out, we have to protect Paul." *Good old Paul,* I thought. I felt the hog twitch and swell deep in my belly; maybe he was going to come inside me anyway. He was grunting hard, but he slid out just in time and shot all over my ass. He rubbed it in with his big hands. It felt like heaven.

I stood, pulled up my panties and tights. I opened my eyes and looked at myself in the mirror; my hair was all standing up as if I had been electrocuted.

There was a loud pounding on the door. "What are you

doing in there?" a shrill voice called out. "No getting high in the bathroom." I put my coat back on and he put himself back into his pants and zipped up. When we went out, the three women standing on line looked at us furiously.

Our beer mugs, now nearly empty, were still on the counter.

"Let me get us a refill," he said.

"No," I told him, "I better get home."

"Home," he echoed in a bitter tone. "Home."

"Good luck with your show," I said. I turned quickly. I couldn't bear to look at him, and made my way through the crowd and out the door.

FONDUE NIGHT

Teresa Noelle Roberts

Chocolate," Antanios said, "isn't actually an aphrodisiac."

"Then why the fondue pot on the bedside table?"

"Because it's fun. But chemically speaking"—he paused to lick a streak of melted dark chocolate from the valley between my breasts—"there are mood-altering compounds in chocolate, but not enough of them to affect you." Although he didn't fit the stereotype with his stocky, muscular build, olive complexion and sculpted features, Antanios *was* a bit of a geek and he remembered weird factoids. "If you ate thirty pounds at once, maybe, but then you'd be in no shape for sex." He dipped his finger into the chocolate and dribbled it onto my nipple. The warmth made me shiver with delight. He'd gauged it well—it wasn't hot enough to burn, but hot enough to get my attention. "It's just so…"

I buried my fingers in his long dark hair and used it to steer his mouth toward my chocolate-dipped nipple. Antanios groaned at the firm touch and got down to business.

His mouth felt almost cool at first in contrast to the chocolate, but it heated up quickly, with delicate licking, then nuzzling, then enthusiastic suckling that drew my soft flesh into his mouth. He bit down hard enough that I felt the sharpness of his teeth and clenched in response. We both like a little roughness, both win when we play control games.

One of his hands explored my other breast, caressing, then pinching and twisting, sending jolts of pleasure through my body. I wasn't sure where his other hand had gone until it reached my lips, two fingers laden with chocolate. This was my first taste of the dark, silky mixture he'd been using to decorate my body. He'd laced it with Chambord. It was so heavenly that for a second I forgot that I might want to do something more erotic to his fingers than just enjoy the flavor.

His hint was about as subtle as my earlier one had been: he made fucking motions with his fingers. The nerves in my tongue responded, sending signals to my pussy. This hit some of the same oral-fixation buttons as sucking cock, but his fingers were much more agile, stroking my tongue, tickling the sensitive spots on the roof of my mouth. Add chocolate and rough nipple play to the mix and I was dripping wet.

Antanios poured more chocolate on my breasts, dipped his fingers again and returned them to my mouth. By the third or fourth time, my face was smeared with chocolate and he was fucking my mouth with four delicious fingers, stretching it wider than any cock ever had. My nipples were hard knobs, delightfully tender from the attention.

I wanted more, and I told him so. I was rewarded with warm, molten chocolate on my belly and his tongue following it, as it ran down to my clean-shaven mound.

Then he licked back up my belly, making sure he'd gotten every drop.

I went for his hair again, trying to direct his tongue where I so desperately needed it, but Antanios just laughed and pulled away. "Spread your legs wider," he ordered hoarsely. When I didn't comply fast enough, mostly because my brain was having trouble processing simple English sentences, he shoved my knees apart. The hint of force made me even more aroused.

He put a pillow under my ass, then knelt back and enjoyed the view. "You are so wet." His voice was almost reverent. "Your lips are all pretty and pouty and slick. I should get a mirror so you can see—but that would take too long."

Being spread like that, open and vulnerable and on exhibit, was making me even wetter. My clit felt like a dick, like I could fuck someone with it, it was that hard. And I would fuck his mouth with it if he'd let me.

I couldn't even beg coherently, but I made an animal growl from somewhere deep inside me and gasped, "Please."

He reached for the little spoon we'd been using to stir the chocolate and filled it. He tested one drop on the inside of his wrist, licking it off with showy pleasure. Then he dribbled chocolate onto my clit, one rich drop at a time. It felt much hotter on the delicate tissue than it had on my breasts and belly, but good hot, the kind of hot that kicked my desire into overdrive, like hot wax, only better because it was chocolate and chocolate is, well, lickable. I was quivering, on the edge of explosion.

Then he began to lick it off and I did explode. When he plunged his fingers into my pussy, replicating the movements he'd used to tease my mouth, all I could do was arch my back and buck against his eager tongue and hands. The sensation was almost too much—almost, but not quite, that fine line where ecstasy crosses over into agony and right back again to a higher level of pleasure.

When the room came back into focus, I was cradled in his

arms, sticky and spent but very, very happy. "Is there any chocolate left?" I asked.

He leered at me. "Ready for more?"

"Oh yes," I purred. "More chocolate, that is. I find I'm a little...hungry."

GLORIA

Jordan Castillo Price

This single-story block of a building that's my home away from home is remarkable only in its blandness. Two doors, a buzzer and an intercom outside. That's it.

Inside, not much more. The main room's pretty much empty, but that's okay. There's only one reason anyone comes here, anyway—the hole in the far wall.

A little sliding door at waist level separates this room from mine, but I usually leave it open. The hole itself is about half a foot square, just big enough for the lower part of my face.

I do a quick check, anxious to begin though nobody ever comes here before sundown. There's not much to clean up since the clients are all women, and women are discreet about these things. But I give the chair a quick spritz of Pledge and wipe down the handrails next to the hole anyway. It's those personal touches that keep the girls coming back, I think.

I go to the mini-stereo in the corner and switch on some background jazz, wordless meandering stuff, and then let myself back into my private room. There's more clutter back here than there is in the front end of the business: takeout wrappers, an old comforter, that kind of stuff. I used to have a neon beer sign but I had to ditch it, since I didn't want any flickering lights calling attention to the man behind the curtain.

I get myself situated, sticking my gum in an old pop can and stealing a glance at the clock. Nearly nine. And just as I wonder how business will be tonight, the buzzer sounds.

I hit the TALK button. "Who's there?"

I lean on LISTEN. I can hear breathing, faint over the ambient noise of a car passing. Someone's there, but it could be anyone.

Probably a customer, though. Sometimes it takes them a while, especially if it's their first time. I don't repeat myself, I just hold down that button. And after a good minute the girl outside answers.

"Gloria."

That's the magic word. They're all Gloria.

I buzz her in.

I hear the outside door shutting and the rustle of her coat as she lets it drop. She stands there for a minute, but I can wait. I haven't closed that sliding panel, but I don't peer through it. That's not what it's about, me peeping at them. Not by a long shot.

She fiddles around, turns the music up. Another pause in which I can feel my pulse starting to surge, and then she approaches the hole. A few twenties folded together slip through, falling into my lap. And then she presses toward me.

I wish I could savor the moment, but this Gloria's new and I don't want to give her second thoughts by making her wait. I rest my chin on the ledge at the bottom of the hole, careful that my eyes don't show, and I wait. Something about giving her my mouth and nothing more helps Gloria let herself go.

Her clothes smell like crisp night air and a hint of detergent, and the sound of her zipper opening sounds like a riff in the background jazz. There's some motion on her end, and soft, wet warmth presses into me. I have a split second of disorientation during which I try to figure out what, exactly, that is.

And then a tongue grazes my lips.

I hadn't expected a kiss—not from a first-time Gloria. But I open my mouth to hers, letting her lead. Her tongue whispers along my lower lip, and her mouth presses gently into mine. Her lips are full and lush, and she tastes a little like cinnamon.

I hear her hands moving over her clothes, getting herself hot, and my cock swells inside my sweatpants. I don't touch it. I want to save my attention for Gloria.

She sighs as she breaks our kiss. She's gotten her shirt open and slides her skin over my lips and tongue, a silky span of warmth from her throat, a hot cleft between her breasts, a soft expanse of belly. I flick my tongue over her navel, wetting it, teasing it.

Gloria's shaking a little now. She raises her body up—I can picture her grasping the handrails, arms straining from holding herself there so taut and still. My tongue trails lower as her body lifts, parting the mound of fur between her legs. It slides between the fleshy lips, flicking over her clit.

Gloria gasps at the feel of me in her now, my tongue probing the contours of her pussy—not dripping wet, not quite yet, but hot and salty and starting to get slick.

She rocks her body against the hole and I tilt my chin up so that I can drive my tongue deeper. I run it up and down the length of her slit while Gloria gets hot, slippery. Her moans come low and breathy, so quiet I can barely make them out over the music.

I reach for her clit with my tongue, but each time I brush

against it Gloria tilts her hips up a little more. She must want my tongue inside her, deep inside her, so I start thrusting it toward her cunt.

She rides my face, fucking it with slow grinds of her hips, and I keep my tongue hard and pointed, making it writhe inside her wet tunnel as her body starts quaking.

I'm ready to feel her pussy start pulling at me as she comes, her opening squeezing at my tongue while her breathing goes ragged. But she pulls back.

I'm confused; then her salty, wet heat presses into my mouth again, wiggling there, begging to be licked. I flicker my tongue out, reaching up for her clit to bring her back to that shivering brink again. But her clit's not there. I find a wrinkly pucker instead.

My cock jumps to attention. It's dying to squeeze past such a tight opening while I grab handfuls of Gloria's bottom and push.

But no, that's not the game we're playing. If I want to fuck Gloria's sweet ass, it's my tongue that's gotta do the job.

Her slit's dripping now, her juice running down so that I can taste it on my tongue and mix it with my own spit. I run my tongue over her ass with a touch so light she might not even feel it. Except it's sensitive down there, and she sure as hell feels it—her whole body tenses, and I hear the whoosh of her sucking in air.

I graze her hole again and her bottom presses into my mouth. I lick her harder, lingering to swirl my tongue over her ass pucker, salty like her pussy but with a hint of earthy sweetness. I feel her shudder. I point my tongue and I push in.

Gloria cries out. My cock's aching and finally I grab it, fisting it right through my pants. I thrust my tongue into her and she pushes back, humping my face with her ass.

That tiny, musky hole contracts around my tongue, squeezing it. I can feel Gloria's fingertips bump my chin as she fingers her pussy, and the thought of her fingers inside her makes heat rush straight to my balls.

She presses her ass into me even harder. I stop breeching her with my tongue, and instead wrap my lips lovingly around that sweet, hot hole. Teasing it with just the very tip of my tongue, I start to suck.

Gloria squeals and her hand gets frantic, both flicking her clit and thrusting deep into her wetness. My tongue tip is busy, stroking, swirling, while my mouth makes hungry slurping sounds at her hole.

I jam my hand down past my waistband and grab my cock, skin on skin, and work it with my fist. My nuts tighten up and my head gets light.

And then Gloria's screaming, not words but a long howl of pleasure. I press my tongue as deep inside her as it will go, and feel her ass pulsing around me as she comes, bucking her bottom against the square hole in the wall.

My own strokes on my cock dwindle to a distracted petting as Gloria's ass moves away. I hold myself there at that brink as Gloria puts on her coat. It's a high, floaty feeling, backing off like that when I'm so far along. But it feels good to be so damn stiff, so turned on.

I hear the outer door shut as Gloria leaves. I miss her a little already, savoring the taste of her ass on my lips.

I contemplate reaching for the lotion and finishing myself off, but the buzzer sounds again. I hit the TALK button. "Who is it?"

A different female voice answers, breathy, maybe even a bit naughty. "Gloria."

I forget about the lotion and turn my attention back to the little square hole in the wall.

PERFECT

Sharon Wachsler

My Master is good to me. She arranges butterfly pillows under my knees and ankles so that my legs can be spread open—my feet high—all day, and my muscles stay loose. My calves do not cramp.

My Master believes in rope, in simple things she buys at the hardware store: slick, strong cords that won't splinter into my skin, chrome-plated pulleys, and thick eyebolts she screws into the walls after she tracks down the stud. She drums the mallet gently against the plaster, listens for the hollowness to become hard and sharp. I anticipate that sound, the stud. I know what it is to feel that hollow, to wait for my Master's hard, sharp hand to find me, fill me, faultlessly.

My Master's ropes are extensions of her arms: they wrap around my chest in a figure eight, pushing out my breasts so that my nipples lick up to taste each passing current. Her ropes sluice up my arms and tie my wrists over my head. But she places more pillows beneath my arms and hands, so I am pure and supple in my submission. I flush beneath the bindings.

My Master believes in thoroughness—in my legs, my breasts, my wrists being held motionless. I cannot squirm, and now, for us, the ropes are the cause. We make my bindings the reason I cannot disturb the perfect position she has set me in.

She brings me water and tea, cradling my head to set my lips against the cup. When she feeds me she cares about what is soft, what is hard: wedges of plum, fresh slivers of raw salmon, her nipples, her fingers, her dick. She is immaculate with the blender and magics my meals into frothy milkshakes. We know how to suck, each sharing the same straw, back and forth, so that when my tongue wraps around the tube, taking it from her, she sees what I can do. In this way she allows me to tease her, because my mouth is awake to every nuance of movement and texture and taste. My mouth is my most alive place. My tongue never tires of pleasing her. My mouth is the freedom we celebrate.

My Master already knows about the catheter. Before, it was for play; now it is for necessity. We use it so that I am always available to her desires and to my body's needs. This is another way in which my Master is perfect: her demands free me from my body's; my restriction becomes delicious. We enact my limitations as her will—vanquishing the power of doctors' diagnoses and of the frequent failure of my muscles and nerves to do my bidding. Our bodies' needs caress each other.

My Master adores my body with ritual. Every evening we bathe, anointing me with oil. She braids my clean hair so that it lies wet and heavy against my neck. She grabs my noose of hair and pulls my mouth against hers. I gasp. I gasp. I gasp.

My Master performs a sorcery of stirrups and cushions. I am open and yielding on the silver sheets, shivering in the heat. She stands with her hip against my jaw while she straps on her acrylic dick. It is rigid and cool. I try to lick the rippling head but she rocks back. I eat my Master's dick with my eyes.

My Master runs lube over her dick and against my swollen lips. I cry out when her fingertips brush my clit. It feels like it has been years since she has touched me, although it was just yesterday. Time stretches me in this bed. I beg for her fulfillment.

My Master lowers herself onto me—her ribbed white shirt pressing against my breasts—and plants her hands below my pillows, thrusting deep into me. So cleanly she slides the head of her cock, rolling it against the roof of my cunt until she owns me completely.

It is impossible to be still now with this wildness in my cunt, this confident intensity on my Master's face. Her dick rubs my spongy inner clit, making me want to yank at my bindings, to snatch at the small hairs at her nape—goddammit!—to clasp my ankles around her waist. But I cannot. Thus I scream her name and bite her jaw. She rears back, pulls her cock to the outer edge of my cunt. I howl. My Master rams back in and against me, grabs my hair and forces her tongue to the back of my throat. My Master is so good to me. "Don't bite," she growls, "or I will stop fucking you." I hold still, because my Master is good and she wants me to come.

When my Master rocks against me, again and again, I feel my orgasm mounting, my true gift. We are raw now with sweat and slippery with lube and come. We ache against each other. Heat races to my center, radiating out from her cock, warmth pouring inside my belly and breasts, legs and toes. My Master is filling me with her complete demand and I scream out with giving it to her. I cannot afford to relinquish any pleasure.

Deliriously we stick to each other, unraveled, cooling. I kiss my Master's neck, her collarbone, her shoulder, the hollow at the base of her throat. She breathes against my ear, my cheek;

kisses my hair, bites my lower lip until it is swollen.

We curl together. "You are perfect," she says. I am good to my Master.

THE WRITER'S MUSE

Gwen Masters

It was three in the morning, the hour when anyone who didn't work the night shift and had any sort of sense would have been asleep in bed. But the muse comes calling when she wills, and in those wee hours I was sitting in front of my computer. Writing, of course. Writing about the man who was lying in the bed just down the hallway.

Why in the world would a woman want to be in front of a computer instead of lying beside her man? When the woman in question writes erotica, sometimes the acts between the sheets have to make their way onto the computer screen. And so I was putting into words all that we had done in the last few hours. The tiny clicks of the keyboard slowly pulled me into the story as my memory ran wild.

I didn't hear him get out of bed. But suddenly he was there, peeking around the corner at me with an indulgent smile.

"You better be writing something sexy, girl."

I smiled up into his blue eyes. Bobby stood calmly at the

threshold of my office door, looking rumpled with sleep. A seam from one of the sheets left a strange reddish mark across his chest. His hair was a mess. His jaw was scruffy with a two-day beard. I watched as he rubbed his eyes and moved closer to me.

The lounge pants fit him just right. They rode low on his hips, drawing my eyes down his body to the place I had been so interested in an hour before. I watched as he read a few sentences of my latest story, quirked an eyebrow at me and asked, "So, who is that lucky guy who got the ride of his life?"

I snickered, and he ran his fingers through my hair. The motion sent a shiver down my spine.

"I like it when you write about me," he said softly.

"I like writing about you."

"I like it when you let me satisfy you like that," he said, and nodded at the words on the screen.

I grinned. "Want to do some satisfying right now?"

Without a word, Bobby slowly spun the chair around. He sank to his knees. The fact that I was wearing nothing but a T-shirt was suddenly foremost on both our minds. His hands settled on my thighs and his teeth settled on the hem of that shirt. His eyes met mine as he grasped my thighs firmly and pulled me to the edge of the chair. I grabbed the arms of the chair and clenched the cold leather in my hands. It quickly warmed under my palm.

"Bobby…" I breathed, an instant before he went to work in earnest. There was no teasing, no careful prying. No hesitation.

"You are so wet," he whispered in amazement. He pushed my knees farther apart. The feel of his breath on my belly made my whole body quiver. Delicious slickness wandered over my clit as he pulled my lips apart for better access. The stubble on his face prickled a little against my thighs, almost tickling. "So wet…"

"I've…been writing," I managed to say, and he slipped one

finger into me. He pushed it as deeply as he could, then slowly pulled it out and lifted his hand to my lips.

"Taste," he demanded, and I did. I tasted musky and sweet, like nectar of a late-autumn fruit that just fell off the vine. Bobby slid his finger slowly in and out of my mouth, mimicking what he would be doing with his body if he weren't down there...on his knees...doing the wicked things he was doing with his mouth and tongue. I bucked up involuntarily when he gently nipped at the hood of my clit, and he shifted his weight forward just enough to pin me to the seat.

I wriggled under him. He held firm. When I slipped my hands into his hair, he growled in warning but he didn't stop me. I sucked on his finger with seductive wantonness. The scent of sex filled the little room. I thought briefly of the light on the desk...the curtains open on the bay window...the fact that anyone walking by might be able to see, were they so inclined...and then I didn't give a damn one way or the other, because his hands were everywhere and his mouth was right where I needed it....

"God, Bobby...I'm going to come...."

He growled with a different kind of emotion and slid two fingers deep into my pussy. I heard his gasp of breath when my fingers tightened in his hair, but I was too far gone to care. I came hard, almost pushing him away as my body bucked and convulsed underneath him. The whimper that ripped from me told him I was too sensitive, and suddenly there was only his breath on my hip, and his fingers moving slowly back and forth inside me. He gently trailed his lips across the inside of my thighs.

I opened my eyes and looked down to see his oceans of blue, dancing with waves of delight. I began to laugh, the chuckle coming from deep inside as he slowly pulled his fingers away. I threw my head back and let the laughter go. He kissed his way up my belly, his lips caressing my skin through the T-shirt I wore.

"Get down here with me," he said lovingly.

I wrapped my arms around his shoulders and we both tumbled to the floor. The carpet wasn't thick and plush, but the office variety, hard on the knees. Bobby had the perfect solution: strip the T-shirt off my body. The air was cool over my skin as he pushed the T-shirt gently under my knees. "Thank you," I whispered impishly, looking back over my shoulder at him.

"You're welcome," he whispered back with a grin.

"However can I repay you for the kindness?" I said, still whispering, slowly rotating my hips in invitation.

"I see two distinct possibilities," he said, and I laughed out loud.

Then his hard cock was against my clit, slipping through the wetness, and I was breathing too hard to laugh. The combination of the story, the teasing, the sight of him between my thighs while I came, it was all just too much. My body was suddenly raging.

He slipped in slowly. One inch at a time. Then he slowly pulled out. It wasn't what I wanted, and I very loudly told him so. His laugh bounced around the room.

"Impatient, aren't we?"

I bit my lip as he slid in one more time. Then he slid out. Then he waited. I squirmed to get closer to him, which didn't work. There is a tightrope between sexual tension and sexual fury, and I was suddenly walking it.

"Just fuck me!"

He chuckled. I lost it.

"Bobby, damn you, fuck me! I mean it!"

"Oooh, she means it," he singsonged.

I tried to move away from him. His hands on my hips were

firm and I didn't go anywhere. So I pushed back into him. My hips hit his. His cock almost slipped in, but he moved just enough that it didn't. I was getting hornier and madder by the minute.

"Please!" I hollered, and before the echo receded he had a change of heart. The thrust impaled me and drove me to the floor. I lay under him, gasping for breath while he pounded hard and fast.

"This what you want? Is this what you were writing about?" he hissed in my ear.

"Please—"

"Why are you begging? I'm giving it to you."

"Too hard," I gasped.

"Too late," he chuckled.

The protest did no good. Bobby went at me with a single-minded purpose. I squirmed and wiggled underneath him, trying to find a position that got him even deeper. More...a little more...and suddenly he hit that spot that made my whole world explode. My orgasm took my breath away.

Bobby sank his hands into my hair and his teeth into my shoulder when he came. He thrust as deep as he could and held very still. "Like that?" he whispered in my ear as his orgasm began to fade.

"Just like that," I whispered back, then smiled. Bobby gently pulled me up from the floor. His lips on mine were soft and gentle as he guided me back to the chair. Through sleepy eyes I looked at the computer monitor.

"Get back to work," he told me, and when I turned for one last kiss, he had already headed back to the warmth of our bed.

Get back to work. I closed my eyes for a moment, then opened up a new document and began to type. *It was three in the morning...*

STUDY BREAK

Jolene Hui

My fingers inched up her creamy thighs under her skirt.

"I have to finish this, Steph," said Justine, her long black bangs falling across her smooth pale forehead.

I let my fingers continue creeping up her inner thigh until she smacked my hand away.

"I said I have to finish studying!" She shifted in her chair so that she was facing away from me.

"I know you need a break...." I stood up behind her and gently lifted her silky hair off her shoulders and moved it to the side. Her tight neck and shoulder muscles softened when my breath grazed her skin, my lips delicately brushing her. I moved them along her neck and down to her shoulder where I shifted the collar of her shirt.

I could feel her giving in, her back relaxing into the chair. Her skin tasted of peaches and cream, the lotion she used every morning. The tinge of sweat glazing her skin made my pussy damp.

My tongue ran up her neck to her ear, where I sucked delicately on her lobe. My hands went over her shoulders and down to her full breasts trapped in her dark corset. Justine liked to dress in black goth clothes, with her hair dyed black and black eyeliner around her pale blue eyes.

She moaned softly and I ran my hands across her nipples and felt them harden at my touch. Her fingers gripped her textbook. She had given in and would have to abandon studying for now.

Justine was taking the bar exam the next month and had been studying for weeks straight. She needed a study break more than anything and I needed to touch her and taste her more than I needed to go to sleep.

"But I..." Her eyes were still closed as I went around to her front and knelt in front of her. The skirts were heavy, but I could lift them enough to sneak my head underneath. She squirmed as she felt my breath on her, nearing her black lace panties. Her pubic hair was light brown—she wasn't really a black-haired beauty. My teeth went straight to the lace and tugged forward. I could taste her juices as I used my fingertips to fully tug off the panties. My lips went directly for her inner thighs first, but then the heat and smell of her arousal pulled me into her clit, which I started to lick delicately. I used my fingers to spread her lips wider. With my other hand, I slipped my middle finger inside her and moved it slowly in and out. I sucked at her clit and worked the fingers in and out at a quicker pace.

Her breath came quicker and her cunt started to pulsate—I'd brought her off quickly. I came up for air to find Justine's hands in the drawer beside her—grabbing my favorite dildo. My jeans were off before she had the toy greased up. I straddled her skirts as she slid the dildo inside me. I leaned forward to put my lips to hers. Her mouth tasted even sweeter than her pussy. Her hand and my pelvis worked in a similar rhythm. My breasts were pressed against hers. I came hard, my juices flowing onto her dark skirts. I moaned and licked her cleavage as I continued to come on her.

As I put my pants on, I said, "Now get back to studying, you naughty student."

A TRUE STORY

Cate Robertson

He's above me, looking down, a distracted smile on his face. Distracted because he's up to the hilt inside me, surging gently in and out while I rock with him.

He loves to watch himself fuck me. He lifts his hips, draws his cock out so that just the tip remains in my cunt, then sinks back into me. Again. And again. I could take this forever. But his gasps turn me on so much that I go after him with my hips. He grins and holds himself back, making me grind up against him.

Then his eyes twinkle wickedly. With his right hand, he reaches down around and slides his finger into my crack. Finds my asshole. Circles.

No. Don't.

Yes.

He presses gently. Suddenly I'm opening. He thrusts his finger in full length. I flinch and wince. Then he starts to move his hand in the same rhythm as his cock, and I break a sweat. I'm going to come hard and fast.

I wake up. Dazed.

He's snoozing away over on his side of the bed. *Fuck*. It was so real.

I'll leave you to imagine where my fingers were.

FROM BITTER TO SWEET

Andrea Dale

Taste: Bitter

I saw you with your new girlfriend today. The one you so unceremoniously dumped me for.

I found your favorite vibrator the other day while I was cleaning, and being the honorable person that I am, I wrapped it up to return to you. I even included a bar of your favorite Green & Black's extra-dark chocolate.

Is it my fault I forgot and let the package sit on the dash of my car on a hot summer's day?

Filling: Nuts

We reached for the last bag of peanut M&Ms at the same time. My first thought was disappointment, but then I looked up and saw her smile as she suggested we split the bag. We sat on the pier watching the sunset, and I was less interested in the candy and more interested in the way she slowly sucked each smooth piece into her mouth, the way her legs stretched out before her, long and lean. Her toenails were painted M&M blue.

I picked out all of the green M&Ms and set them aside. She raised an eyebrow; she knew what they meant. When we finished eating and the sun had set, I offered them to her.

She set one on my collarbone and nibbled it off. I felt the sensation of her gentle teeth all the way down between my legs. She suggested we share the rest of them at her place, in private.

Texture: Creamy
Her skin is dusky like toffee, smooth like caramel.

On our fourth date, she set up a fondue pot full of semisweet Hershey's morsels, hot and liquid. She dipped strawberries in and fed them to me, holding one end between her full lips and kissing me through the confection. Eventually we abandoned the fruit. She said my nipples were like plump raspberries, and bathed them in melted chocolate before sucking on them.

Later, she told me about Ben & Jerry's Super Fudge Chunk, and what she would do to me with it.

Topping: Marshmallows
I said I hated camping, but she convinced me to go for just one night. Over the crackling campfire, she made real hot chocolate—not powdered, not from a mix. Mayan Hot Chocolate, she said, slicing the chilies and splitting the vanilla beans.

After we drank it, she dragged me into the tent. The burgundy nylon rustled as we evoked the pagan gods and sacrificed ourselves on the altar of our lust.

Taste: Sweet
She slips the chocolate pastille—some astonishingly expensive kind from Switzerland—into my mouth. The dark, sweet taste explodes on my tongue.

"No biting," she instructs. "You have to let it melt. And you can't make any sound until it's all gone."

My tongue screams, but I don't, even as she moves her way down my body. I writhe and sweat, but remain mute like she asks. My world turns dark red, like the inside of a chocolate-covered cherry.

Green & Black's no longer seems exotic.

I've almost forgotten your name.

BART AND RANDI

Michael Hemmingson

"Fuck her," Bart said. "I want to watch you fuck the shit out of her."

Lying naked on the bed, Randi smiled.

I was with them, the both of them, in Bart's apartment, but I wasn't quite sure how I had gotten there. Earlier, we'd been at the pub. We were having a good time, and Bart found it amusing that I was sleeping with a certain mutual friend.

"Funny? Why is that so funny?" I asked.

"She doesn't seem your type," he said.

"My type?"

"Yeah."

"What's my 'type'?" I asked.

"You tell me. Take Randi, for example."

She was a few feet away, talking to someone, and she couldn't hear us.

"Okay," I said.

"She looks good."

"Yes."

"Nice ass."

"Yes."

"Nice tits."

"Yeah."

"She's fuckable," Bart said.

"I imagine so."

"Sucks cock goooood," Bart said.

"I imagine so."

"Is she your type?"

"She could be my type," I said.

"You want to fuck her?"

"What kind of question is that?"

"*Listen,*" he said, "I like watching guys fuck her. It really turns me on."

So then we were at his place, and Randi got undressed and sat on the bed.

"Who would've thought," Bart said, laughing, and slapped me on the back.

I wasn't sure what he was getting at.

"C'mon, fuck her." Bart pulled up a chair.

Randi did look good. They were both beautiful and blonde and tan. While Bart was a "surfer poet," Randi worked as a hostess of some upscale club downtown, and I knew she made good money at it. I could not help but feel aroused, especially looking at the blonde pubic hair between her legs.

Randi noticed what I was gawking at and opened her legs. Her finger touched her clit, and made a circular motion. "You like what you see?" she said.

I did. I went down on her, engulfed her, got a mouthful, got a taste, ate her. I put my tongue in her as far as I could get it. I was about to turn her over when Randi started pulling at my pants, saying she wanted my cock. Bart was getting a real kick out of this, sitting in the chair, drinking a Heineken. I was on my knees on the bed and Randi was reaching around, cupping my balls with one hand, squeezing my ass with the other, and sucking me off. Then I was fucking her. I fucked her several ways, and came.

"Right on," Bart said.

Bart got on the bed, and I sat in the chair. I watched Bart kiss her, watched as he started fucking her, his ass going up and down. He had a perfect, round, tanned ass. Randi spread his ass with her hands, and said, "Hey, would you like some of this?"

"Crazy woman," Bart laughed.

"I like watching men fuck him," she said, "as much as he likes watching men fuck me."

"I don't think our pal swings that way," Bart said.

"Do you or don't you?" she asked me.

I got up, and went to get a beer from the fridge. Bart continued to fuck her.

Later, I wondered if I should have fucked Bart after all. I was in the mood for anything.

PLEASING

Jocelyn Bringas

've been thinking...."

Uh oh, Clayton thought when he heard Jacelia say that. She looked so somber.

"About what?" Clayton questioned as casually as he could.

"About us,"

Oh fuck, she's gonna break up with me. Fuck, fuck, fuck.

She sighed, "It's just that I feel like a horrible girlfriend," she said quietly as she looked down at the ground.

Clayton stared at her, stunned at her confession.

"I shouldn't have said anything," she stammered. "Forget it."

"You're an amazing girlfriend," Clayton insisted, once he'd found his voice. "Why would you feel that way?" It baffled him that she would ever doubt herself.

She blushed. "I just heard you talking with Erik. He was saying how he had just gotten a great blow job, and you were saying how it's been so long since you've gotten one. I know we have plenty of sex but I've just never... I just felt so bad."

"Oh, well it's nothing to feel bad about, baby," Clayton said.

"Yeah but—"

"What?"

Jacelia closed her eyes and said, "I really want to suck you."

Clayton's breath caught. Jacelia had never talked like that before. Just hearing her say those words aroused him. The truth was, Clayton was pretty content with their sex life. In fact they seemed to have made love in every position possible, aside from oral sex.

"You can do anything you want to me, baby," Clayton whispered before pressing his lips to hers.

Jacelia's glossy pink lips moved against his as they began to kiss. Clayton moaned when he felt her hand over the front of his jeans. Rapidly, he felt himself getting harder from her simple touch.

"Come here," Clayton said breathlessly, momentarily breaking the kiss so they could move to the couch. Clayton sat down, watching as Jacelia got naked and then knelt between his legs, rubbing her palms against his thighs.

Jacelia's fingers crept up to the button of his jeans. Soon that was undone and in a matter of seconds his pants were unzipped, yanked off, and tossed away.

Clayton watched Jacelia stare at his dick in both fascination and awe. The wait was aggravating. He just wanted her to suck it, but he knew better than to rush her. "Oh god," Clayton groaned, his head falling back against the couch as he felt her cool hand wrap around his hardness.

"I've had this inside me but I've never really looked at it," she said, her warm breath touching his dick, making him twitch.

"Uh-huh," was all Clayton could manage, not really caring

what she was saying. His hips moved up, wanting more pleasure.

"It's so smooth, too," she said as she started to move her
hand.

"Oh, fuck," Clayton panted, feeling a warm mouth encircle
his tip.

Opening his eyes, he looked down to see Jacelia's head going
up and down, concentrating on pleasuring him. It felt so different and so good to be in her mouth. Her tongue licked along the
underside of his dick, hitting pleasure points he never realized
he had before. Clayton groaned as her hand grazed his churning
balls. This was just too much for him, being in her warm mouth;
he was going to come soon.

"Jacelia," he moaned, feeling her movements grow faster
now. Her lips were sliding up and down furiously on him. He
could feel the pressure starting to build up in him as she sucked,
licked, and kissed his dick.

"Baby, I'm gonna come!"

Clayton inhaled and exhaled loudly as he was hit with a tidal
wave of pleasure. He arched his back and pushed his cock even
deeper into her mouth as he exploded and came. Jacelia was
momentarily shocked by his sudden orgasm and pulled away,
but she quickly recovered, taking him back into her mouth and
jerking him as he kept shooting. When he had ridden his orgasm
out, he caught his breath and opened his eyes.

Jacelia's face, neck, and full breasts had his come all over
them. He was surprised at how intense his orgasm had been. He
watched as Jacelia wiped some of his juices off her nipple with
her finger and brought it to her mouth, tasting it.

Just seeing her drenched turned him on, and he felt himself
get hard all over again. He had to fuck her. Standing up, he mo-
tioned for her to do the same. He let his hand go between her

thighs, feeling her soaking wet pussy. She moaned as she started to grind herself on his palm.

"Bend over," he instructed.

Jacelia placed her palms on the cushions of the couch and stuck her luscious ass out for him. He rubbed her smooth cheeks and spread them, preparing for entry.

"Fuck me, Clayton," she pleaded in a little-girl voice.

Clayton didn't need any more encouragement to slide inside. She was so tight. It made him proud to know that he was the only one who had ever entered her. Gripping her hips for leverage, Clayton began to thrust himself into her, loving the sweet pleasure he was receiving. Faster and faster he went.

"Oh, it's so good," she moaned.

Clayton drove into her, his skin slapping against hers creating a sweet sound.

"Come for me," he encouraged, taking a hand off her hip and reaching around to rub her pulsating clit.

"Oh, yes," she whimpered, feeling his fingers move over her clit. He started to feel her orgasm build, and he knew this was his cue to go faster, and he thrust even more.

Clayton groaned as he started to come inside her and he felt her shuddering with her own climax. When their orgasms subsided, Clayton pulled out and took her into his arms and held her.

"You're amazing," Clayton whispered, "and no matter what, you always please me."

She smiled at him, looking both relieved and satisfied. He smiled back, lifted her up in his arms and carried her up to their bedroom to sleep.

SATURDAY AFTERNOON STEAM

Joel A. Nichols

Every Saturday morning, I'd roll out of bed and stumble into my red nylon shorts, the taste of beer still in my mouth. None of my friends could figure out why I would want to lifeguard at the school's natatorium on the early Saturday shift, but none of them knew how busy the sauna room got once lap-swim was over.

The lifeguard station consisted of a tall chair just outside of the long hallway that led to the men's lockers. Sometimes I brought a magazine in case of slow mornings, but within an hour the first jocks would come to cool off after a workout. One Saturday, four hockey players pumped up from the weight room had run from the lockers, naked. I watched as the four beefy guys dove in and took half a lap each, laughing and jostling each other in the pool. Then they turned around and pulled themselves out of the pool right in front of me, only a bit sheepishly considering their flopping cocks and dangling balls. Three disappeared behind the lifeguard chair before I'd really seen much more than a blur of brown and tan flesh. But one guy took his time.

As he hauled himself out of the pool, his biceps tightened and pulled the rest of his torso up over the side, uneasy on the wet tiles. I leaned forward in the chair and took a better look. His shoulders were thick, his pecs hairy, and a solid stomach led into the groove of his hip. My cock started to get hard, but there was enough room in my red-lined shorts. The hockey player had a tattoo of a horned devil on his right shoulder, the shoulder that was turned my way. With both feet out of the pool he straightened up and looked right at me.

I blushed and turned away.

I could hear his friends scampering up the tiled hallway, and he started behind them. I looked again and caught another glimpse of his cock, drooping forward. I'd crossed my arms over my hard-on, and pressed my forearm against it. It sent shivers up and down my legs, even in the overheated pool area. The four naked guys disappeared into the showers. Now there were only two older professors left in the pool swimming laps, completely unaware of the spontaneous peep show or my tightening erection.

I heard a dull thud and a cry of pain. I craned my neck and looked up the hallway. The lingering streaker had slipped on the wet tile and lost his balance. He swore again, and grabbed at his ankle.

I climbed down from the chair and started toward him, slowly. The front of my shorts was still tented, and I tried to rest my hand on my hip to hide it.

"Fuck," he said. He lay sprawled on the floor. He'd pulled himself almost into a sitting position, his back against the wall. He was rubbing his left ankle.

I knelt down next to him. He tried to cross his legs to hide his cock, but as he moved his left side, he winced in pain. "You shouldn't run in the pool area. The rules are posted." I loved giving him my lifeguard lines, as if he were a rambunctious child at the neighborhood pool.

"My buddies and I dared each other to run in bare." His voice was deep, unsubtle. He scratched his leg, then moved to stand up again. I put out my hand, and he grabbed it. My dick jumped, and his twitched as it swung with his body. I wanted to grab it, but he let go and stepped back. "Thanks."

He walked the rest of the way into the shower room, his muscular ass jiggling with every limping step. I walked back to the pool and climbed back up the chair. I noted the slight injury in the log, smiling at the thought of his naked body. My dick got hard again and I rested the clipboard on top of it, creating a slight friction around the rim of my cock. I couldn't wait for my shift to be over. When the pool closed on Saturday afternoons, and most of the gym emptied out, the steam room got hot. There was usually some discreet action in the fog of the sauna; I'd once gotten a blow job from a guy in his midthirties, a young professor or coach or something, and I'd jerked a lot of different guys' cocks, from student athletes to plain old cruisers. The sauna was my reason to work the pool on Saturdays.

My shift wore on, the sagging professors swimming with remarkable ease and proficiency turning lap after lap. I glanced occasionally at the magazine I'd brought in between long, attentive sweeps of the pool. My dick went up and down when I thought about the hockey player, about his friends jostling in the showers, probably soapy and wrestling.

The last swimmer hauled herself out of the pool, and I headed into the sauna.

The guy who'd fallen was still at the showers.

I stripped off my shirt and shorts, kicking my plastic sandals into the corner and turning toward the sauna door. I wouldn't have to wait long.

THE MAGAZINE

Bonfils

I came home from work early. As I opened the door to the living room, I heard the hurried shuffling of papers.

Brandi sat on the sofa, her face flushed. She stared at me with a confused expression on her face.

"Anything wrong?" I asked.

"No…" she said, smiling nervously. "Why?"

But then I looked at the coffee table. And there it was, sticking out from under the newspaper: the colorful corner of a glossy magazine.

"Been reading?" I asked, grinning.

Brandi bowed her head, blushing.

"C'mon," I said. "Let me see." Slowly, she pulled the magazine out and showed me. It was one of my porno magazines—and one of my favorites.

Brandi knows I like porno, and if she wanted to see the magazine, she'd know where to find it. But she'd never helped herself to it before. At least, not to my knowledge.

"So," I asked. "Which story did you like the best?"

Brandi leafed through the magazine, looking at the spicy photos. Naked men and women engaged in outrageous acts of lovemaking graced every page.

"This one is quite sexy," she said shyly.

She showed me the magazine. It was a photo series of two men tying up a girl and giving her a serious fucking. Really hot. It had always turned me on, but I was surprised that Brandi would pick that one.

"That's a good one."

Brandi smiled. "Well, the girl seems to be enjoying it," she said.

The guys were really giving it to the girl in all sorts of poses. My cock was beginning to stir and swell. Somehow, Brandi holding the magazine made it even sexier. She looked really cute today in her pink blouse and blue jeans. Actually, a couple of buttons were undone. Had she been masturbating when I came in?

I took the magazine from her and looked through the story. "Take your clothes off," I said.

Brandi stared at me nervously for a moment. Then she stood and began undressing. Her blouse came off, exposing her shapely breasts; then her jeans, and finally her black silk panties. She stood naked beside the couch looking gorgeous.

"Come here," I said. "On your knees."

She knelt down in front of me, and I unzipped and pulled out my cock. Brandi opened her mouth and closed her lips around my cock. She began sucking rhythmically, teasing it with her tongue, making my erection grow and harden.

"Yeah," I whispered.

Brandi sucked me vigorously, moving her head back and forth. My member stiffened, filling her mouth. I grabbed her hair and began pulling her head back and forth, controlling the rhythm, as my eager cock impaled her mouth with each stroke. She could make me come by sucking me—and she often had. But I had more in store for her today.

I pulled out of her mouth.

"Take the magazine," I gasped, "and get down on all fours."

Brandi did as I said, her cute little bottom turned toward me. I knelt down behind her and gently brushed my finger across her pussy lips. She was wet. She was really wet.

As I stroked her pussy, she moaned quietly with pleasure. Gently, I pushed the tip of my finger in between her lips. I felt her body trembling slightly.

"Now show me your favorite picture."

Brandi's hands were shaking as she leafed through the glossy pages of dirty pictures. I kept softly stroking the mouth of her cunt.

"Oh god…" she gasped, dropping the magazine.

Her other hand was now playing with her breasts, caressing and pinching her nipples. Brandi only does this when she's very excited. And I guess she was. I heard the pages rustling, as she tried to find the page she had been looking at before I came in. Finally, she made up her mind, and pointing to a photo, said: "Here… This one…"

I looked at the picture. In it, the girl was wedged between the two men. They were all naked. One man was fucking her ass, the other her cunt. The girl had her head thrown back, apparently crying out loud in ecstasy. A pretty rough picture—and it was Brandi's favorite. This was really starting to turn me on.

I assumed the position behind her ass. "You like that?" I asked, still fingering her pussy. "You'd like to be that girl?"

"Ohhh," she sighed. "Oh yes."

As I slowly slid inside her, I was so excited, I could hardly breathe. Her pussy felt so good around my cock. Slowly, I began to thrust into her, deep and hard, feeling her succulent cunt clenching around me. She moaned lustfully every time I entered her.

I grabbed her ass, kneading her shapely buttocks as I kept pumping. I looked down to see my cock slipping in and out, stretching her with every stroke.

"Read to me," I gasped. "Read from the story."

Brandi whimpered with pleasure, then began to read, gasping for breath every once in a while: " 'Tracy screamed with lust...as she felt Marco's cock...inside her ass. He thrust his giant pole into her...like a madman. As the two enormous cocks...filled both her holes, she almost...fainted with lust....' "

Excited as hell, I increased my pace, driving my cock into Brandi's pussy in a frenzied rhythm.

"Yeah," I said, "keep going."

Her whole body was trembling, as she read on: " 'Tracy's cunt was...slippery with love juice. As the two men...savagely fucked her, she...came again.' Oh god!"

Like the girl in the story, Brandi came. Overwhelmed by the lustful sensations, she thrashed about on the carpet in her climax. I held on to her hips and kept right on fucking her, deep and hard.

"Keep reading," I gasped.

Breathing deeply, she composed herself. Still shaking, she took the magazine and read on: " 'Tony's cock was...ready to explode. He thrust deep into her pussy...and Tracy...felt him... pumping into her cunt.' *Please...* 'She screamed with pleasure as Marco unloaded...into her ass.' "

"Oh, yes," I murmured, pulling my cock from her. I, too, was ready to come. I grabbed my cock in one hand. "On your back," I commanded.

Brandi rolled over, her glazed eyes staring at me.

"Play with your pussy," I told her.

Obediently, Brandi began stroking her tender pussy. She whimpered with pleasure. Holding my cock, I straddled her, placing my knees on either side of her body, working my cock hard in my fist.

"I want you to come again."

Brandi increased her pace, her body trembling with pleasure, as we masturbated together. "I'm coming, baby," I moaned, climaxing onto her. Brandi whimpered, and I could tell she was coming, too. Afterward, I stood up, exhausted. Brandi just lay there, savoring the afterglow of her second powerful orgasm. Then she looked up at me, smiling.

"You know what I'd like to do now?" she asked.

I shook my head. But somehow I knew what was coming. Brandi reached for the magazine. "Let's read another story."

HOW TO SPANK ME: AN OPEN LETTER TO MY FUTURE LOVERS

Shanna Germain

First, leave a note on the bed before you leave for work, telling me what to wear. I'll find it on your pillow when I wake up, and smile when I realize you've chosen the pleated pink mini-skirt, a white baby-doll T-shirt and those bottom-hugging white panties that you bought me for my birthday, three to a package. Suggest, in your carefully crafted scrawl, that I wear heels. I'll know that you mean my three-inch-high strappy black sandals, the ones that let you see my toes. In your PS, tell me that you'll be home at 3:00, and that I'd better be ready.

Be late.

At 2:30, I will parade around the house in my skirt and heels, my nipples popping through my baby-doll T. By 2:45, I'll get into position as instructed, bent over the kitchen table, my hands and elbows pressed against the wood, my ass in the air, just barely covered by my skirt and panties. By 3:00, I'll still be in position, anticipating your arrival with tingling nipples and tingling cunt. At 3:15, I'll notice the cramp in my right calf, the way that my hands are sweaty on the wood, the fact that the crevice of my underwear is soaked and sticking to my newly shaved skin. By 3:30, when you still aren't home, I'll convince myself I can't stand it any longer, that you're not coming, that I'm going to go back and put on sweats just to spite you. I'll consider masturbating, just to relieve the ache that's building up inside me.

Walk in the door at 4:00, just as I'm about to give up, just as the heat in my panties has grown cold, just as I don't think I can stand it any longer. Step up behind me. When I turn my head to look at you over my shoulder, when I open my mouth to say something nasty about the fact that you're late, say, "Face forward." Say, "Don't speak."

Correct my position without saying a word. Straighten my hands on the wood and make sure my head is down on the table, then push my feet farther apart with your leg. Do it roughly. Flip the short skirt up over my ass, then rub your hands across the panties. Find the wet spot and dig your finger in, tease it there until I lift my ass higher in the air, already begging for it, moaning into the table.

Tell me to be quiet. Tell me that I am not allowed to make a sound until you say so. Stand to the left of me, and reach under my T-shirt and tweak my nipples, first one, then the other. With your other hand, return to rubbing the wet spot in my panties. Realize I am panting and pushing my ass toward your hand, trying to catch as much of your flesh as possible against my skin. Say, "Don't move." Then flick my clit through the material until I am bucking and bucking, unable to keep still.

Let your hand swat my buttcheek, just once, a swift stroke that catches the fleshy part of my ass and makes my head spin. When I cry out, do it again, and again. Threaten to tear off my panties and spank me naked. Tell me what a bad girl I am for wanting it so much. Wait until I'm panting, begging, sticking my

ass toward you again and again, wait until I'm so wet I'm dripping into your hand, and then back off.

Make yourself a cup of coffee. Stand back and stare at my
ass—positioned like two peach halves in the air, barely covered
by my dripping wet panties, just waiting for you. Sip your coffee
while you ease the white fabric down over the cheeks of my ass
without touching my skin.

Get undressed.

Do it slowly, so I can hear every button, every zipper, every
slide of fabric over your skin. Press your skin against mine, hold
my cheeks in your hand, first one, then the other. Feel their juice,
their heft. Moan. Tease my bare slit with your fingers. Keep doing it until I beg. Enter me with you fingers, first one, then two,
then three. Slide them inside me over and over until I'm fucking
your hand, legs spread wide before you, my grunts and moans
covering the sound of you fucking me.

This is your cue: slap the fleshy part of my ass with your
palm.

Alternate. Repeat.

See the blush growing across my cheeks? This same redness
is on my face too—excitement, shame, joy.

Pay attention as you spank me. Note the change in pitch
when I moan, the way I toss my head back, just a little, each
time your hand slaps my ass. I'm about to come.

Stop.

Step back and pick up the belt that's draped over the back of
the chair. Run the leather through my wet crack and across my
clit, until you feel me shiver, until I arch my back, begging for it.
Tell me you'll let me have it if I touch myself. Wait until I take
my hand off the table, press it between my legs, look back over
my shoulder at you, begging.

Take the end of the belt and slap it, softly, against my ass.

So that it makes a noise, but doesn't hurt too much yet. Let me know there's more where that came from. Ask me if I want it.

When I whisper *yes,* slap me a little harder and ask me again. When I say *yes,* slap the other side and ask me again and again, until I'm grunting *please, yes please, yes, yes, yes,* until my flesh is warm and red beneath your hand, until the sound of the belt against my ass is loud, so much louder than my own voice as I arch and quiver and come.

Wait until I am able to breathe again, until I can back away from the table, then hug me against you so I will not fall. Tell me how much you love to make me come. Tell me that it's my turn to be on top tomorrow.

ALLEY OBSESSION

Xan West

I take you to the alley. I know exactly where I want to go. It's dark, but the streetlight isn't so far away that we wouldn't be able to see danger coming. The danger is part of the point. Danger is one of the key elements that make it hot for me. It's not just the public part. That could be at a bar or a dungeon, but fag + public sex = danger. And that amps up the desire for me. Because the risk of getting caught elevates our interaction to a whole other level. It's the danger that kicks it up another notch for me, gets my cock hard.

That's why I chose this alley. Fag friends have cruised by with me, shown me where to go, described protocol. Told me story after story about being on their knees, or getting sucked off, or (if it's especially late and fairly empty) bending over against the Dumpster and getting fucked until their legs are so weak they can barely make it home.

You know the same stories. You're standing there against the wall, strategically placed to watch for danger. You're a cocksucker's dream, every inch the leather daddy of my fantasies. At first you pretend you don't even see me, as my eyes devour you in your leathers, a big butch bear, built just how I like my daddies to be. You take up space, owning it, top to the core as you survey the drooling cocksuckers before you. I am entranced by the sight of your cock in your pants, run my eyes along it hungrily. I am aching to be chosen to service you in any way that you please.

You look into my eyes, hand on belt, stroking your cock through your leathers. Your other hand slowly reaches over and your thumb brushes against my lower lip. You raise one eyebrow at me as your hand presses firmly on the top of my head. No words are needed. I am instantly on my knees looking up at you before I can even think about it. You lace your fingers together behind your head, bend your knees slightly, and settle in comfortably, waiting for me to service your cock.

I take it out, and my mouth is watering as I slip a condom on, getting it ready. I tongue the head, fiercely layering need and anticipation as I savor the feel of your cock against me. I place my hand at the base and start stroking there slowly, just enough to tease. Then I take the head into the shallow of my mouth, tuck in my teeth, and start coming down on your cock, just the head, testing to see how much pressure you want. I am looking up at you through my lashes, your cock in my mouth, as you look down at me and growl, "Yeah, boy, like that. Show me what a good cocksucker you are. That's where you belong. You were born for this. You crave this. You were made to service my cock."

As your words enter me, my cock rises. I start taking your dick deeper into me. Slowly at first, gathering saliva, so I can start thrusting you down my throat. I'm stroking the base of your cock harder now, in time with my mouth's rhythm. I take you into my throat deeply, coming down harder on your cock.

"Yeah, boy. What a good little cocksucker you are. You can do it. Take it all. You know you want this. You live for my cock. It's just you and me, faggot. Just your throat and my cock. You love being a hole for me. That's all you are, a hole for my cock to use. Nothing else. Take me in. Come down hard on my cock. You need to be the best cocksucker in the world. You know how many willing mouths I can find if I just walk a few steps? Convince me you are the best. Yeah. Harder. Faster. Right there, just like that. If you do this right I will take you home and fuck you till you can't move. Show me how good you are. Take it all."

Your words transport me to the zone. I work my mouth on your cock like this was all I was built for. I could go on forever sucking you. The world disappears and it's just me and you, just my mouth servicing your cock for as long you want it. I start to move faster, finding the rhythm of thrusts that will get you off, working my hand at the base of your dick in just the right motion. Your hips are moving involuntarily and a litany of dirty words leave your mouth, becoming growling groans. You are guiding me to come down harder, take you in deeper. Your dick thrusts deeper in my throat than I thought any dick could, deep inside me as you spurt, groaning, with fast thrusts of your hips. You control the rhythm completely as your orgasm thrusts into me, faster, deeper. Your final thrust almost knocks me off balance.

I slowly take my mouth off your cock and lick my lips, looking up at you. Your hand snakes down to grab the hair at the back of my neck and pull me up to face you. You whisper words of praise as your hand touches my cheek, then my forehead above my nose. You pull me in for a kiss, gently at first, and then fiercely, biting my lip. You work your mouth along my throat, tongue the base of it, feeling the fluttering heartbeat. You drag your teeth along the vein, biting, then sucking, then biting even harder. Your cock is brushing my thigh as you pull away from my neck to tongue my ear, wrapping my hair around your hand and pulling my head where you want it. I feel your breath as you whisper gruffly, "Come on, boy. Daddy's got a lot more he wants to do to you tonight."

WATCH AND WAIT

Justus Roux

Julie finished tying Derek to the chair then carefully placed the silk scarf over his mouth and tied it tightly behind his head. She looked over her masterpiece, then ran her fingers through his soft blond hair. Never had he looked so inviting as he did now. The ropes had been carefully placed over his well-sculpted body. Her eyes drifted down to his cock. He was already hard and ready.

"Nice, very nice," she purred. She leaned over and licked the head of his cock.

Sweet anticipation filled the air. Derek had requested this and Julie was more than happy to oblige him. She stepped out of the closet and closed the mirrored door. Derek could see everything behind this door. Julie stood in front of the mirror and slowly took her clothes off. She squeezed her breasts, then wetted one of her fingers and rolled it over her erect nipple.

The sound of the doorbell caught her attention. "Ready, baby?" she sighed, running her hands down the mirror.

Julie went to the door. Derek could hear the muffled sounds of conversation. He shifted a little in his chair. He groaned when he saw his best friend Jacob enter the room right behind Julie. There was no mistaking that look of lust on Jacob's face. What man wouldn't have that look with a beautiful woman strolling around naked? Derek's heart beat harder as he watched Julie slowly undress Jacob. He had mentioned to Julie that he often wondered what Jacob looked like fucking. No wonder this was the man she had picked to have sex with while Derek watched. Derek's cock throbbed when Julie came to her knees in front of Jacob.

"Where's Derek?" Jacob asked, grabbing a handful of Julie's hair.

"He's all tied up at the moment." She licked at the head of his cock.

"When is he coming home?"

"He won't be coming for a while." Julie smiled at the mirror as she ran her tongue down the length of Jacob's cock.

"God, you're beautiful," Jacob groaned pushing Julie's head closer. "I could watch you suck me all day."

"All day, huh?" She looked up at him as she took his cock deeply into her mouth. Her nose nuzzled his pubic hair as she managed to swallow all of him.

Jacob's moans and the delicious image displayed in front of Derek were driving him crazy. He wanted to fight with his restraints, to free his hands so he could stroke his cock. But he couldn't risk Jacob hearing him, so Derek bit down on the scarf as he ached for release.

Jacob reached down and pulled Julie up to her feet. "I want to fuck that tight little pussy of yours."

Julie climbed on the bed, then lowered herself down onto her elbows. She lifted her ass into the air. Jacob hurried over to the bed and grabbed her hips. With one forceful thrust he buried his cock to the hilt.

The position Julie had placed herself in gave Derek a nice view of Jacob sliding in and out of her. This was torture, but sweet, delicious, torture. His eyes took in everything. The way Jacob held tightly on to Julie's hips as his eyes looked at her beautiful ass. Derek shifted in his chair again. His eyes traveled up Julie's body. Her tits bounced to the rhythm of Jacob's thrusts. That look on her face drove Derek crazy. God, she was so beautiful when she was being pleasured.

Derek's eyes went back up to Jacob when he heard him groan. Jacob tilted his head back and had such an exquisite look of pleasure on his face as he cried out. Derek's cock ached so badly, he needed release. He moved his hands in the restraints but Julie had done such a good job at tying him up there was no way he was going to free himself.

Julie climbed out of the bed. "That was good," she said, licking at Jacob's nipple. It wasn't Jacob's cock that brought her to orgasm. She could feel Derek's gaze upon her and it had caused her body to shudder. "But Derek should be coming pretty soon."

"When can I see you again?" Jacob asked as he put his clothes back on.

"I'll let you know." She escorted him out.

Derek's body ached, but it was so deliciously good. He struggled more when Julie opened the door.

"Is that what you wanted?" She slowly climbed onto his lap, letting her pussy sheath his cock. Slowly she slid up and down, squeezing her pussy tightly.

Derek's head fell back as his orgasm rocked him. It was so powerful it almost hurt. Julie undid his gag and kissed him deeply.

"Untie me," he whispered against her lips.

She did as he asked, then grabbed his hand and led him over to the bed. Still hard, Derek lunged at her and pinned her to the bed. He held her arms above her head as he thrust his cock into her. He rode her hard and rough, driving faster and deeper. The sound of their bodies slapping together filled the room.

"Baby," Julie purred, holding him close to her. "I would say you liked our little game."

"Next time, you'll have to watch and wait," he said as he ran his tongue over her lips.

Julie bit her lip lightly as her body quivered with the thought.

TRANSFORMA-TIONS

Jen Cross

After you leave my apartment, you always go to the twenty-four-hour gym. There, you lower yourself onto the padded bench, narrowing your hips and shoulders to fit its length, and push up hard until your biceps sing with strain and sweat beads at your temples.

But for now, you're strung out on the rumpled sheets of my unmade bed, and your girlfriend would never recognize you. The buttoned-up butch girl you are in public has become a drenched mass writhing under me. I kneel between your spread legs, pressing my thigh into your hot cunt, with my hand as far into your mouth as I can get it. It's taken a good half hour of dirty talk and gentle twisting and pressure to get into you this way, and your eyes are glassy with strain. Hoping I don't notice, you rotate your hips slightly, trying to increase the friction between your clit and my leg. I do notice, though: this display of your need makes me grin.

Slowly, I extract my little fist from behind your teeth and you

cough, glaring at me with all that longing you're so ashamed of:
you hate to be a girl, and I turn you into one. I turn every little
bit of you into a cunt. Worse, for you, is how you've begun to
revel in this widening of your hips, the rounding of your belly,
the swelling of your ass and your tits. My touch brings out your
curves—which is why we'll never date or even be seen out in
public together.

The birds have just begun to sing morning songs outside my
window. I can hear the earliest garbage collectors thunder and
crash up the street. If they make it in time, they will shout their
appreciation for the screams that rend your throat when you
come. You've been at the edge, just ready to pitch over, for a
long time now. I don't want to let you go. I'm always afraid I
won't be able to catch you—and I never quite do.

I'm so turned on that the slick heat of my pussy has chafed
inside my leather pants. I lost my white undershirt, wanting you
to see the tits that you aren't allowed to touch, while I had you
on your knees, begging for the cock tucked into my pants.

You've stopped hanging out with me at clubs and bars. It's
not that you're worried your girlfriend will find out we're fucking. You're more concerned she, or any of your friends, will see
how we fuck by the way your shape shifts beneath my gaze and
breath.

After you leave my apartment on these Saturday mornings,
you go to the twenty-four-hour gym. You don't look at yourself
in the mirror until the end of your workout, when you're finally
reeling with something besides sex and need.

I turn my now-slick fingers along the just-inside of your cunt,
thereby encircling us with the fragrance of your sex. The gar-
bagemen pass by underneath my window, making no indication
they're paying any attention to us. I've kept you out too long
this time. Your girlfriend will have left several messages on your

cell phone, which you haven't checked since walking through my door.

Your cunt, which always seems so razor clam–like when I first take down your boxers, has plumped with blood, juice, and desire. I snap on a latex glove, grinning again at your flinch, and—painfully slowly—slip two fingers between those fat lips. Now that you're free to cry out for more pressure, you do. It's the first direct caress your cunt has gotten all night and I struggle to make it last when what I really want to do is force every bit of me inside of you.

I will always run our fucks. It's the only way I can pretend I have any power here. As soon as you come, you're gone.

Your stomach tenses when I shove my fingers as far up into you as they'll go, add a third, and then a quick fourth. You wrap your hard arms around my neck and try your best to twist your fingers in my buzz cut. You moan steadily, the sound rising and falling like an approaching emergency. The light filtering into the room through my dirty shade yellows the sheen of sweat on your face. Ungracefully, I use my teeth to pull a glove onto my other hand, and slide the two middle fingers of that hand into your cunt, adding to the fullness already opening you. You groan sharply against the added pressure, dropping into a frustrated yelp when I yank them back out again.

"Lift," I say, my voice harsh with need, and I press up against the top of your cunt, teasing the far edge of your G-spot. Your hips rise smooth and fast, your bare feet firmly planted on the sheets. I slip my free hand under your ass, which has grown from the square hard thing it was when I spanked you an hour ago to a malleable round fruit.

I once tried to describe this transformation to you, but you shut your ears and eyes from acknowledgment. There is to be no documentation of this coming, this lust. Just your punctual,

1:00 a.m., post-Friday-night-partying, knock on my apartment door. And then later, at the gym, you'll hide in the corner machines through the first half of your circuit, tensing those hard and thick muscles against more and more weight. Only when your body is refocused and gleaming do you dare to make eye contact with any of the other early morning gym queens.

"Stay," I say, and ease the tip of my middle finger into your ass. You don't seem to know whether to clamp down against this invasion or stay open to the four fingers pummeling your cunt. It's hard to tighten up one orifice without clenching the other, and you submit to remaining full and loose. I sigh and squeeze my thighs together, trying to ease some of the ache in my own pussy. The finger, oiled by your cunt, slides past the first knuckle, then the second, and gets sucked up through that sphincter.

You press against my chest as a fierce, sonorous orgasm crests and careens through your flesh. You cry out into the quiet of my room, into the slow morning breaking outside, claiming your love for me, and for my hands, in a nearly inaudible voice, one so high pitched it could almost only be heard by other dogs—like me. My ears ring. Even the depths inside your cunt have rounded for me, opened up like the sweetest cave, like the bud before it bursts to flower. You cover my glove with cream and pollen.

You don't sleep. Gingerly, you pull off both my hands, and lower yourself to the bed, stretching out your tensed muscles. You avoid meeting my eye. I watch the next transformation begin, transfixed despite my pain at seeing all my hard work so quickly undone.

It doesn't take long: you disentangle your body from mine, and begin to fold your face up. Your round cheeks, both facial and gluteal, are sucked back to starving. You deprive your breasts of their fullness. You roll away from me and grab for your clothes.

Before you can thin yourself back into your idea of butch-ness, I grab your head and kiss you, with your lips still so thick and swollen from cocksucking earlier. After all these months of Saturday mornings, it's the first time I've tasted the arousal collected under your tongue over so many hours.

You allow yourself to respond for a second—for a second—and then you're gone. You yank yourself out of my grasp and dress so fast I nearly miss it when I turn to the window and blink back the need blurring and burning the edges of my vision. I never am quite sure how you manage to stuff all that flesh into the tight jeans and T-shirts you wear—but you find a way. You cast a disparaging glance over your shoulder—disapproving of my violation of our ritual—then toss your jacket over your shoulder, and leave my apartment door open when you go. As soon as you come, you're gone. The *you* I know. The *you* I fuck you to. The songs you sing when we're together get rolled up and tucked back under your breastbone for no one else to see.

I hear the high, thin voice of your Kawasaki revving, and picture your body bent over and holding on to it like the truest lover. Later, when my own body throbs to orgasm, I imagine you at the end of your set, finishing some hundreds of sit-ups. You rise on stumbling legs and head to the showers, ready to wash away the last remnants of your morning with me.

A NO-WIN SITUATION

Alison Tyler

Tell me about Van."

I flushed and looked down at my breakfast, a fancy fruit plate filled with papaya, mango, pineapples. But although the exotic assortment was beautifully arranged, my appetite had vanished.

"He's the man who showed you what you were really like, isn't that right?"

"No." I shook my head, scared to disagree with him, but needing to explain. "I already knew. He was just the first one who saw what I wanted. Who understood."

"And you idolize him for it...."

I'm not an idiot. I figured out immediately that this was one of Jack's trick questions. Not really a question, even. Yet he clearly expected a response.

"I don't know," I said finally, "we weren't together all that long. It wasn't good all that long. But at the start, it was kind of...magic."

"Why did you split up?"

"He disappeared. He'd told me on our first date that he was in 'importing and exporting.' I hadn't known that meant drugs. I was naïve. And one day he just didn't show up for a date. I didn't hear from him for almost a month."

"What did you do?"

I cut all my hair off. And dyed it fuchsia. I wore his sweatshirt every day. I stopped even pretending to care about what people at school thought about me. I got too thin. I tried to track him down, and his roommate told me to forget he had even existed.

"I mourned him."

Jack stared at me for a moment. "And then what happened?"

"He called me and asked me to meet him at a coffee shop. When I saw him there, I couldn't even go in. I walked away. He ran after me, chased me down, dragged me to a park bench and started to talk. He said that if he'd told me the truth when we first met, I'd never have gone out with him. Probably true, but I don't know. He said he loved me."

"And you believed him?"

I stared directly into Jack's eyes. "Yes," I said evenly, "he did love me."

I knew that if we hadn't been in public, Jack would have slapped me for my tone of voice. Jack's expression hardened, and I swallowed hard but didn't look away.

"You asked me," I said, "and you told me not to lie to you."

"And then what?" Jack pushed on.

"We went to this twenty-dollar-a-day hotel on the edge of town. Creepy place. And we stripped down and messed around. But it was different."

"That was it?"

"No, of course not. It dragged on for a while. We both

pretended that everything was the same as before, yet now he seemed determined to show me that he was broken. And then he disappeared again...and I went off to school...."

Jack nodded, and I felt him memorizing my story. Learning it.

"Tell me three bad things about Van."

I thought I had. "He was a drug dealer. He lied to me. He disappeared."

"No. Tell me three things that you don't like to think about. Three things that fill you with shame."

I tripped through my mental storage and shared what I could. "When he came back, he'd lost his power. I don't really know why. But he had. He begged me to take him back, and it made me cold inside. I despised feeling like that."

"That's one."

"I flirted with someone else in front of him. I wanted to see him get back in charge, and he wouldn't. I couldn't get a rise out of him, and I hated him for that."

"Two."

"He tried to be gentle with me. He tried to show me that he could fuck me sweetly, and it killed me inside. I felt wretched afterward. He couldn't get hard, and I felt as if it was my fault."

"Stupid man," Jack said softly. "He thought he was giving you something you wanted, when it was the last thing on earth you craved."

I nodded.

"Head to the bathroom, but leave the door unlocked."

I stood immediately and walked through the café, to the single restroom at the end of the hall. I turned on the light, and waited. The room was tiled in blue and white, decorated French style, like the rest of the café, with a basket of potpourri and angel-winged mirrors. In seconds, Jack had joined me. He looked at me from the doorway, stared at me in total silence, and then flicked off the light, shut the door and locked it.

I felt my heart racing. We were in inky blackness. A tiny beam of light from the crack at the bottom of the door was the only illumination. Jack was on me in a heartbeat, turning me around to face the wall, lifting the hem of my dress, pressing his body on mine. I could feel how hard he was. So fucking hard. He bit into the back of my neck, and then undid his jeans, slid my panties aside, and thrust inside of me.

"I can see you in my mind," he whispered. "This young girl, desperate. I only wish that I was the one who found you first."

He fucked me fiercely, slamming me up against the cold tiled wall, darkness enveloping us. "I want to know everything about you," Jack continued, his voice low and hard. "I want to know it all."

Again and again he thrust into me, and just before he came, he slipped one hand in front of my body and pinched my clit, sending me spiraling with that glimmer of pain. That spark of pleasure. I pressed my face against the wall as the climax flared through me, and I felt limp as Jack pulled out, tucked himself back into his jeans, and then flipped on the light. He pulled my dress back down, then turned me to face him. I kept my hands at my side, and I stared at him, somehow waiting.

He slapped my face, hard, as I had known he would. I gritted my teeth and stared down at the floor. I deserved it. I'd told him bold-faced of Van's love. But I was trapped in a no-win situation. He didn't want me to lie. Yet he didn't want the truth.

But I'm lying now. No win? Of course I won.

He slapped me, and I had craved the feeling of his strong hand on my cheek. I had tested him for once. I had been bold; cocky, even; and Jack had brought me right down to earth, right down to my place.

No win? With Jack, even when I lost, I won.

Every single time.

HOLLY'S FANTASY

Kate Laurie

I glared up at the clock on the wall. It was nearly ten p.m., and my best friend Lauren had promised to be over by nine in order to help me get tomorrow's orders ready. The only baker I employed had quit two days ago and I had six cakes that all needed to be ready for pick-up by noon tomorrow.

Just then I heard the back door open.

"Thanks for coming, Lauren," I called over my shoulder. A decidedly masculine clearing of the throat made me spin around. Instead of Lauren, a gorgeous man was standing inside the doorway. "Who the hell are you?" I asked as I grabbed a rolling pin. It wasn't much of a weapon, but it was all I had.

He flashed an uncertain smile. "You must be Holly. I'm Lauren's cousin, Michael. She got called in to the hospital, so she called me and asked if I'd mind helping you out."

I was doomed. There was no way a man who looked this great had ever had to cook his own food. He was the type of man that would induce nearly any woman to cater to his every whim. "Have you ever even been in a kitchen before?"

"Aren't you being a little sexist? For your information, I happen to have attended culinary school. I promise that I will be more than you expected." The heat that came from his blue eyes made me think he was talking about more than just his baking.

There was something about his dark hair, or maybe it was those pouting lips, that made me want to drag him up onto my baking table. But the cakes had to be my priority. "Okay, first I have two black forest cakes, a German chocolate, and two of my specialties, Holly's Fantasy." I couldn't help but look at him as I said the last.

He reached over me and grabbed a bowl, slowly dragging his arm across my nipples and causing them to harden immediately. I was going to have to be careful tonight. I really had to get these cakes done. The last thing I needed was a bad review because I couldn't get my orders done in time. Michael seemed to sense my anxiety because he moved to the other side of the table and began following my recipe with an ease that promised he was all he'd claimed.

I took a deep breath and began following his example. The sooner I got done the sooner I could sate the throbbing that had begun between my legs. He looked at me and winked, causing my panties to dampen even more. I glared at him and turned back to my mixing bowl, cracking the eggs with a vengeance.

After that, we worked without stopping. Without talking. But not without flirting.

Two hours later, I leaned back against the table and sighed. I don't think I'd ever worked so hard at baking. I was overheating, and not just from the heat of all the ovens. Throughout the last few hours Michael had been tempting me more and more. Who knew that the simple act of sifting sugar could cause my body to clench up in desperate desire? I looked over at him and felt my mouth go dry. He was sprinkled in chocolate. I had stripped down to my tank top while we were finishing my fantasy cakes, and he had dropped the bowl he had been carrying, causing the contents to splash onto him. He tore off his apron and shirt and stalked over to me.

The man had the most amazing body I had ever seen. I nearly came when he ran his hands up my sides. I rose up on my toes in order to run my tongue along his neck, licking off the chocolate that was beginning to run down to his chest. He shuddered in my arms and then lifted me onto the counter. He pulled off my tight tank, freeing my eager nipples to his touch. He wiped some of the chocolate off of his own chest and coated my nipples with it. Then he set his mouth upon one peak and began to suck with an expertise that made me grind my hips against his. I leaned forward and unzipped his jeans, freeing an erection that caused my clit to swell in anticipation. He let go of my breasts to slide his jeans off and I dispensed with my slacks at the same time.

"You are so sexy," he whispered into my ear as he gripped my hips and pulled me onto his throbbing cock. He began to say something else, but the words changed to a moan as I used my grip on his shoulders to slide him in deeper. We quickly developed an urgent rhythm of desperate lust.

My entire world was made up of the sensation of his strong chest against mine and the velvet steel inside me. I rocked forward and suddenly I was there, gasping as the climax tore through me. My steady contractions around him brought on his orgasm, and I threw my head back in ecstasy as I eagerly milked his cock of all it had. The moment seemed to last forever, and as I finally came back to reality I gasped the only thing on my mind.

"Do you need a job?"

Michael just laughed.

COME FROM BEHIND

Cate Robertson

Sometimes on hands and knees, sometimes on elbows. Sometimes with my face crushed against the bed and my arms flailing, clawing the sheets or pillows. Sometimes forced flat.

Sometimes he grips my upper arms and levers me upright, kneels back to spoon me into his lap, hoisting and dropping me. Grunt work: reverse posthole digging. Sometimes he pushes me down and compresses me, fingers splayed in the middle of my back. Sometimes he caresses me with two hands from point of shoulder to arse, tracing the hourglass: doggy-style accentuates the incurve of waist, the bloom of hip.

Sometimes I take it like a punching bag, thrust along the bed, cheek burning, lower lip dragged open. Sometimes I fling myself backward, feel him pierce me belly-deep. Sometimes I arch my pelvis upward and keep still so that he can watch himself ease thick and wet into me, shuddering. Sometimes, I reach back between and jostle him tenderly.

He gropes for my lips, smooth and drippy: oyster-flesh. He

pinches my little pearl while his shaft strives for my G-spot. Gasping, he tussles with my hips, accelerates, wrestles his orgasm into the open ground of my cunt.

Every time I come, screaming.

SHORT-LIVED LACE

Lynn Burton

W hat about this one?" Janie asked, holding up a white satin and lace teddy.

"Too pure." I didn't want white. To seduce Ryan, I'd need something dark. Something striking. My plan brought a smile to my lips.

"This one?"

I grabbed the chemise—a short spaghetti-strap piece with lace trim and a slit on one side. "Perfect." The black satin was as slick as my panties felt. "Let's get it and go."

Janie led the way to the counter but stopped suddenly, and I ran into her backside.

She turned and looked at me with a gleam in her eyes that I wasn't sure I'd ever seen before. "How about something to go with it?"

I held the material close to my body, moving slowly, seductively, as if dancing. "This little number needs something to go with it?"

Janie answered by handing me a black velvet choker with rhinestones from a display table. She circled behind me and pulled my hair up while I placed the addition around my neck just to see if it'd fit. The light touch of her fingers raised goose bumps on my bare arms. Her hands lingered in my hair as she let it back down.

"*Now* you're ready," Janie informed me.

By the time we reached the parking lot, my insides ached with want, but not for Ryan anymore. My original intended plan vanished as soon as we got to Janie's car.

She opened the back driver's side door and said, "Get in." I wasn't about to argue.

She climbed in beside me, reached in the shopping bag and pulled out the choker. "Put this back on."

With the choker in place, Janie slid closer and kissed me. Her lips were soft, her tongue probing. Her hands roamed over my neck, my hard nipples. My skirt was now an obstacle and she tugged at it in frustration.

Stilling her greedy hands, I quickly removed the skirt and she moved in to delve her fingers inside me. One finger. Then two. In and out. Slowly at first, then picking up speed. Up to tease my swollen clit, back down to my tight entrance. With her free hand, she found the chemise and ran the material over my sensitive mound.

It was enough to almost make me come.

Janie pushed my shaky legs open wide and went for my neatly shaved pussy as if it was going to be her last meal. She made those hungry slurping sounds, licking, biting. Her green eyes met mine for a moment as she murmured, "You taste so good," and then went back to her feast. I slipped my hands through her hair, encouraging her to take all she wanted. And she took—all of me—slow and steady, fast and hard. My hips bucked against her attentions and a rush of heat pooled under my naked ass. Her mouth could've become permanently attached to my pussy and I wouldn't have cared. As long as I got to taste her, too; and I had a feeling my turn wouldn't be that far in the future.

When Janie slid back up the length of my body, we kissed for a long time. The taste of my sweet honey lingered on both our mouths and I knew I held the best laid plans in my arms.

SALACIOUS ROBINSON

Sylvia Day

Hello, Mrs. Robinson."

I can't stop the thrill that courses through me at the sound of the familiar deep voice. But then, I don't want to. I'm horny, and he knows.

"Hi, Jason." I turn away from my husband's tool bench in the garage. The weather is hot; summer in our town always is. Today it's at least one hundred degrees. Suddenly, it feels hotter than that.

My neighbor's son stands shirtless in the driveway; his baggy shorts hang low around trim hips. He's not wearing boxers, and a shiver races through me despite the heat. His cock, which I know to be long and thick, hangs heavily, tenting the cotton khaki of his shorts. I lick my lips.

"How are you today?" he asks, stepping into my personal space.

I look past him. His truck is the only car in the driveway next door. "Fine. My kids are napping. I just put them down."

His full mouth curves seductively at the words he'd wanted to hear. He comes closer, his powerful athlete's body rippling with muscle. I love to watch him move, watch him play. His mother is my friend. I've sat next to her at his college football games. I've sat next to his girlfriend, too.

Jason brushes past me, his shoulder deliberately skimming across my nipples, making me ache for him. He hits the remote on the wall and the door begins to lower, blocking out our neighbors. Before it's halfway down, his shorts are on the floor. By the time the door is closed, he's not the only one naked.

My blood races in my veins. I love the cock he's fisting, I love it fucking me.

His smile is smug. My desperate desire is why he comes to me. He knows how bad I want it, how deprived I am. My need strokes his ego as surely as his cock strokes my cunt.

I jump up onto the edge of the pool table and spread my legs. I'm dripping for him, and when he gets to me, he slides right in. My eyes close, relishing the feel of the hot, hard, huge cock inside me. I lift my heels to the table, opening myself completely. Leaning back on my arms, I slit my eyes to watch him. That's all the stimulation I need, the sight of his youthful body, full of grace and strength, glistening with sweat and lust as he pumps deep into me.

As he holds the edge of the table and thrusts hard and fast, his six-pack abdomen ripples with his exertions. There's no time for foreplay or finesse. There never is, but I don't want either one. I want to be fucked.

I moan; I can't help it. He feels so good. The thick head of his dick stretches, massages, and rubs the inside of me.

"Like that?" he grunts, driving deeper.

"God, yes."

I gasp, arching my hips to take more. The friction is amazing.

There's nothing like the feel of being fucked by a big cock. I tell
him so and he growls. He loves it when I talk dirty; his girlfriend
won't. She's too young, too inhibited. I have no shame.

Sweat dampens his hair and drips down his chest. The delicious scent of hardworking male fills my nostrils. It's so unbe-
lievably hot in my garage with the door closed. Like a sauna.
He's breathing heavy, his body working hard. Jason never has
any control when he takes me and I make it worse by moaning,
by loving his cock as much as I do.

"I'm going to come," he warns. He fucks like a stallion and
climaxes like one, too—hard, deep, and copiously.

I whimper, wanting it, my nipples so hard they ache, my
breasts heavy and shaking with the impact of his hips slapping
against mine. His dick swells in anticipation, filling me so full he
really has to work to get inside me. The pleasure is incredible.

He floods me, still fucking madly, and I orgasm.

"Yes, yes, yes," I chant. The release of the sexual tension that
knots my shoulders and back is so good, I shake. A moment later
he stills; his head dropping forward as he catches his breath.

Five minutes later the garage door is opening and a dry, hot
breeze blows in, evaporating the perspiration from our skin. The
sound of an automobile door shutting nearby alerts us to arriv-
als.

Jason's father is home and stepping out of his car. I wave. He
waves back.

"Thank you for your help, Jason," I call out as he saunters
away, his back glistening in the summer sun.

He doesn't glance back. "Any time, Mrs. Robinson."

BACKROOM SALLY

Inga Mahn

R ight back here, just follow me, Mama will show you where
the real fun is," the saucy old madam taunts.

She hears the footsteps, she hears the voices, as a customer is
led into her booth, but all she sees is darkness.

"So, I can really touch her then?" the stranger asks.

"Oh yes, you can touch, you can do whatever you like, as long
as you keep dropping the coins in." The old woman cackles.

She wiggles her body in the uncomfortable seat, spreading
her legs wider to give her customer the best view of her bare and
ready cunt. She hears the door close, and the sound of the man
clearing his throat. She hears the sound of the coins jangling in
his hand. Finally she hears the *clank clank* of a coin dropping
into the slot, and the snap of the one-foot-by-one-foot window
opening between her legs. Then the *clank clank* of another coin
as he enables the speaker that allows her to speak to him.

"Oh yes baby, you wanna fuck my pretty cunt?" she asks.
"You wanna stick your fingers deep inside it?"

She hears him groan.

"Oh, touch me baby before the window closes, fuck me baby." She continues her well-rehearsed dialogue.

Before he gets up the courage to touch her the window snaps shut.

"Oh baby, please, I need to get fucked," she continues before the speaker cuts out.

Clank clank. More coins fall into both slots.

"Oh yeah baby, you gonna fuck me now, you gonna make me cum?"

Now he touches her. Rough fingers shove deep inside her, twisting and shoving at her flesh.

"Oh god, that feels good. You're gonna make me cum, oh yeah, just a little more," she continues before the window again snaps closed.

He barely pulls his fingers back in time. A string of curses fill the small booth.

Clank clank. More coins fall into the slots.

"You gonna fuck me now? Come on, fuck me hard," she taunts him.

"Oh, I'm gonna fuck you good now, bitch," he says.

His cock jabs at her opening.

"Oh yes baby, that's how you do it, fuck me baby, fuck me more," she moans.

She blocks out his rough prodding. Silently counting in her head, she feels her cunt suddenly begin to pulse with excitement. Three, two, one...the window snaps closed. He howls in pain, and her hips buck off the seat as her orgasm washes over her.

As the speaker cuts out he hears her sadistic giggles.

SHE LIVES ALONE

Kathryn O'Halloran

She lives alone. She likes it that way, likes her dainty dollhouse with ornaments dusted weekly then realigned with precision. On Sundays, she washes unstained floral sheets and sips tea from a delicate china cup. No yearning for lust-sodden skin ever breaks the elegant surface.

But sometimes she misses the smell of a man.

At night, a lingering ghost licks at the edge of her olfactory senses. She awakes, gulping in air, drawing it to her but never quite succeeding.

On the train, on the way home in peak hour, she presses close against strangers. She inhales deeply. But it is unripened, this scent of city-tame suit-wearer. What she craves is a particular mix of sweat and sex and man.

She hunts through neon and hidden alleys, guided by her need. The air is thick and stale, like beer the morning after pay-day. She is exposed, alone and female. She sits alone on an un-steady stool. Stares at a bubble gurgling through a bottle behind the bar and picks at her fingernails.

She orders another drink.

The music turns to disco, the lights pulsate, flashes of red and pink and green. She flicks the edge of a laminated cocktail list. She knows she can leave at any time. She knows she won't. Stares ahead.

She orders another drink.

He stands beside her, ripe and waiting. She turns, expecting conversation, but he is silent. He mumbles something as she turns away. She turns back and he is gone. She clinks the ice in her drink with her straw.

She orders another drink.

She sits in the toilet cubicle, pants around her ankles, paper in her hands. Her head spins and she tries to focus on the writing on the back of the door. So many people, so many loves. Who does she love?

He stands at the basin when she comes out. She ignores him while she runs cold water over her hands but she knows he is watching. Their lips lock before their eyes do. He is diesel and pine shavings and sweat from heavy manual labor that a thousand showers cannot wash away. She will succumb. She will abdicate. She will grind and moan on cue.

Later, dressing in the half-light, she knocks a glass off the bedside table. She pauses and hopes it doesn't wake him. Clothes askew and hair unraveled, she is ready for flight. In the doorway, thoughts become actions before they are fully formed, although she would deny that this is what she came for.

She runs through unfamiliar streets, stunned at her gall. At the bus stop, oblivious to the stares of strangers, she unballs the T-shirt in her hands and holds it to her nose. She inhales deeply.

RESEARCH

Kate Vassar

The reference librarian looked up from the computer monitor and smiled, one of those long, slow smiles with a lot of
eye contact. She was a tall, slim Amazonian goddess with short
blonde hair, dressed in a boring suit that she managed to make
look good.

I tried not to stare.

"Excuse me," I said, "but I'm writing a paper on librarian
stereotypes in the movies, and I was wondering if you could
help."

Was I blushing? Yep, I sure was. How obvious could I be?

"I'm Sara." The librarian held out her hand and I took it, an
electric spark of attraction traveling up my fingertips and pulsing through my entire body.

"Lucy." I couldn't believe I remembered my own name. I noticed she was looking at me like I was doing something odd, and
I wondered what it was. Then I looked down and saw that I was
idly caressing the wood of her desk, and blushed even harder,

ducked my head, and stopped.

She smiled at me reassuringly. "Well, Lucy, let's see what we can find," Sara said. "It's an area filled with negative stereotypes." She rolled her eyes companionably, and I had to smile.

"You ever think that...maybe that 'old maid' librarian was really gay?" I stammered. Sara looked into my eyes with a knowing smile, and I could tell she knew exactly what I was asking. "Yes, I think that's a definite possibility," Sara replied.

Score!

When my notebook was filled with citations, I said, "I think I have enough articles here for...coffee?" Sara raised a curious eyebrow, and I hastily explained, "Would you like to get some coffee?"

Why did I invite her out for coffee? I barely drink coffee!

Sara smiled, a slow, broad, sexy smile that I felt in my knees and stomach. "Would you rather have a beer at my place? I get off at five," she said. "Meet me out front?"

"Okay, yes, definitely." I was vaguely horrified at my complete lack of suavity, but her smile got even bigger so I grinned back, then gathered up my notebooks and left.

I rushed home, and spent just a little too long trying to come up with the perfect outfit. I finally decided on a long, loose skirt, tank top, and sandals. Then I rushed back to the library.

"You mind if I change out of my work drag?" Sara asked as we went in her front door.

"Not at...no," I said.

While she changed, I looked around at her apartment and tried to figure out how I was going to make my move. I'd never seen so many books outside a library! I supposed I could read to her out of her volume of Sappho, but she probably had girls doing that all the time. How *do* you seduce a gay librarian?

Sara returned in jeans and a muscle shirt, revealing some of the sexiest biceps I've ever seen. "Pete's okay?"

"Um, sure," I said, settling onto the couch with a complete lack of finesse.

She returned with two beers, sat next to me, and handed me one. She took a long sip, then said, "May I ask a question?"

Uh-oh.

"I was just wondering if you were planning on seducing me."

I stammered something lame.

"I was just wondering," she continued, "because I figured that if you weren't going to seduce me, maybe I should seduce you." Then she leaned over and kissed me.

Ding ding ding!

"Well," I admitted into her soft, lush, delicious, faintly beer-tasting lips, "it did occur to me to read Sappho to you, but I figured you probably get that a lot."

"I never get that," Sara said with a rueful smile.

I moved to hop up with the plan of grabbing the volume, but I never got that far. Sara pulled me into another knee-melting, spine-tingling kiss. It was a spectacular kiss, like receiving a powerful electric shock, only pleasant. Then my brain switched off, leaving my lips and hands happily in charge. I gleefully peeled off her tank top to reveal that she wasn't wearing a bra, and I went into a kind of active swoon, my mouth finding her soft pink nipples. She moaned, and somehow managed to get my top and bra off, I still don't know how. I moved up to kiss her again, hands fumbling blindly with her jeans, and she laughed gently and helped me out.

Boxers! Oh, baby!

She slipped a hand under my skirt, and discovered to her apparent delight that I wasn't wearing underwear. I was also probably in danger of soaking through her couch, but I didn't care. My lips were still everywhere they could reach, but my hands were desperate to explore the contents of those boxers, and I heartily approved of my hands' plans.

Unfortunately for my hands but fortunately for me, she had other ideas. She knelt on the floor in front of me, hooked her hands behind my ass, and pulled me to the edge of the couch, flipping up my skirt and glancing upward mischievously before bending her head to lick me. I wrapped my legs around her head and hoped I wasn't squishing her ears until I just couldn't think anymore.

"Oh god," I said, not even caring if that was a clichéd thing to say.

She grinned at me and wiped her mouth with the back of her hand, then kissed me again. "I was thinking about doing that all day, but I don't think the library wants me picking up girls on the job. I'm so glad you asked me out."

"When do I, um, get to find out what's under those boxers?" I asked, blushing.

"Is that a research question?"

"Yep."

"Well," she said, "I feel it's my duty to help you satisfy your curiosity."

That was good, because I had a feeling I'd have lots of questions.

THE WINDOW

Aimee Nichols

Alone in her bedroom, Cecilia strips naked. Despite the long, mundane and seemingly endless week, she is horny, prowling through both her bedroom and her mind like a hungry tigress, searching for some inspiration—any inspiration—to feast off.

She stalks to the window and shoves the curtains apart, feeling a vicious thrill as they nearly tear from their rings. She unlocks the window and flings it wide open, letting the world in and exposing herself to the warm night air that surrounds her body. Her nipples harden and she marvels at how the breeze almost seems to suckle at her breasts. The air could be her lover; it moves across her naked form like a hundred tongues, exploring with delight the topography of her body, coaxing her skin into gooseflesh and letting her allow herself to tremble openly from its ministrations. The wind is her most shameless of lovers, worshipping her and wanting to selfishly possess her at once.

She snaps from her reverie and scans the front garden, taking in the moonlit shadows of the plants and trees that hover among the branches and spread themselves across the lawn. She notices how the path leading to the front gate segregates them. Her garden is bushy, dense and unkempt; messy and wild like Cecilia would be if she let herself. The area near the front fence is particularly concentrated; it looks impenetrable.

Cecilia likes to think that people can see in even though she can't see out. Cecilia likes to fantasize that someone's out there, watching her, as she pads around her bedroom getting ready for bed; while she lies on her bed reading at night, naked and carefully arranged to give her imagined voyeur the best possible view. She's excited when she thinks that just by lying there, she might be the object of fantasy for some silent observer. She watches porn videos with the sound turned right up and the window open and imagines that the man she's invented, the man who's out there lurking in the bushes on her front lawn, is watching his own porno inside his head as he masturbates over her.

Cecilia mounts the windowsill, dangling her legs over onto the cool brick, and allows the air to caress her. She perches with the knowledge that she could be visible to anyone. Slowly, solemnly, and with great relish, she begins to touch herself.

Zack wanders down the street, wondering where his disdain for suburbia has taken itself tonight. All he sees are endless rows of houses like boxes, trees, shrubs and concrete driveways. He doesn't know what's wrong with him. He's too old for ennui; too young for a midlife crisis. He feels so listless, like there's no point to anything. Nothing and no one holds his attention for long. He hangs his head and watches his feet walk, convincing himself he's fascinated by the dragging of his footsteps. He hears a noise coming from the house he's walking past, and his head turns abruptly. It sounds like some kind of animal crying out, and he wades through the bushes in front of the fence, his curiosity piqued. He is stunned at what comes into his view: a woman perched on a window ledge, legs flung wide, head thrown back, body in total surrender to her fingers as she touches herself, occasionally dipping inside to retrieve the moisture she is producing in plentiful amounts. He feels himself grow hard as he takes in her breasts with their erect nipples, her wide-open legs, and the fingers that play so skillfully with her own body. His cock throbs as the slick wetness on her fingers and pussy catches in the moonlight. He unzips and releases his cock, taking it firmly in his hand for the only time in months that hasn't been to urinate.

Cecilia is close to perfect bliss. Her body tenses, waiting for the leap into ecstasy that it knows is inevitable. She no longer knows or cares if anyone is watching her; all she can focus on are the sensations her body is producing. She trembles, then as orgasm hits her body, rocks hard against the sill, so hard she risks falling into the garden. A howl of release escapes her throat and a dozen neighborhood dogs reply. Her panting is loud and ragged, easily distinguishable from the front of the garden where Zack comes into his hand with a hot pent-up jet.

Simultaneously, Cecilia and Zack sigh and come down from their clouds.

Simultaneously, they accept their normal worlds, each unaware of the great service he or she has done the other.

THE BEST CURE FOR JET LAG

Teresa Noelle Roberts

B y the time Lisa and Andy got through Spanish customs, found a cab, conveyed to the cabdriver where they were going (Andy finally resorted to digging the hotel brochure out from their carry-on and brandishing it under the guy's nose), and made it to their hotel, the last thing Lisa felt like doing was playing tourist.

Sleeping for a week was much higher on the list.

Maybe coming straight to Barcelona from Chicago, after all the sleep-deprived nights leading up to the wedding, hadn't been such a great plan. But of course they hadn't listened to the smart people who'd suggested spending a night in a nice hotel in Chicago being pampered before the long transatlantic flight. Oh no, go straight to Spain and start having fun! It had seemed like a good idea at the time. Of course until she actually went through the whole event, she couldn't conceive how exhausting and stressful being a bride could be.

It didn't help that Andy was wide awake and eager as a golden retriever who wanted to go for a run. He hadn't slept much either—certainly not on the plane, where they'd been seated right behind a colicky, miserable baby—but blessed with a crazy biological clock that seemed to thrive on stress and lack of sleep (very useful for a programmer) he'd hit a high instead of a low.

"Hey, you can see the cathedral from the window. Want to check it out?"

"Is there coffee between here and there?"

He peered out the window again. "There must be coffee somewhere. We're in a major city. Let's go."

She tried to answer, but yawned instead. "How about a nap first?"

"Can't nap. Then the jet lag will get us for sure. Come on, you'll feel better if you keep moving. Unless you meant a 'nap' instead of a nap." Finger quotes and a lascivious grin made it clear what Andy meant by the first "nap."

She managed a smile. He looked so cute—her sexy, silly Andy—she'd have loved to jump him and start the honeymoon off right. If she lay down, though, Lisa knew she was done for.

"You trying to kill me, babe? I haven't even had a chance to change my life insurance yet." She put her arms around him, gave him a big kiss, just enjoying the comfortable way their bodies fit. "Maybe if I take a shower…"

Andy nodded. "Good idea. I'll see if I can get some coffee from room service."

The bathroom was surprisingly spacious and nongeneric, outfitted with what looked like Majorcan tiles, and the water pressure was blessedly high. A good shot of cool water woke her up a bit. Gradually, she turned it up to steaminess, reveling in the sense that the grime of travel was washing away. She imagined the layers of exhaustion from days of poor sleep and weeks—make that months—of wedding-planning wackiness were melting away with it.

She might live.

The bathroom door opened. Andy walked in, shedding the last bits of his clothes on the floor as he entered.

"Coffee's coming," he said as he slipped into the shower. "Told them to just leave it since we'd be showering. I figured I should make sure you don't drown, being so tired and all." He took the washcloth out of her hand and began soaping her back.

By the time he started lathering her breasts and belly with the rich, herb-scented shower gel, Lisa felt much perkier. She leaned back against him, feeling his cock pressing against her, enjoying his fingers working her slick nipples and wandering down to swirl between her legs.

Once he rinsed the soap off her and knelt down to lick drops of water from her clit, exhaustion was the furthest thing from her mind. She braced herself against her husband's strong shoulders, driving her nails in as the pleasure rolled up and down her body and came to rest against where his tongue played. And when she thought she couldn't stand any more, that her tired body would simply collapse from the combined forces of hot water and hotter pleasure, Andy stood up again, his hands running along her body, and turned her around so she was facing the wall. There was more hot water running over her sensitive skin, and the scent of herbs. Andy's slick cock slid in and out of her drenched pussy, fingers on her clit circling in time with the thrusts, and she pushed back onto his length, swaying her hips, grinding against him then pulling away to make the next stroke feel deeper. It wasn't clear to her if she ever really stopped coming from the time he was licking her until the moment he slipped out of her, sated, or maybe even a little after that.

The aftershocks continued, mild but delightful, as she cleaned away their mingled juices.

Just in time for the soft knock and the welcome sound of coffee arriving.

"Now," Lisa said, "I think I'll be ready to play tourist."

NAILS

Bonnie Dee

Aidan lifted Delia's heel in the palm of his hand and applied a stroke of rose polish to the nail of her big toe.

"Don't you dare spill that on my bed." Delia nudged him in the hip with her foot.

"I won't if you quit kicking me."

He overlapped several more strokes of color, blew lightly over the nail, then kissed the top of her foot before starting on the next toe.

Delia closed her eyes and concentrated on the minute feeling of the brush tickling her nail and Aidan's hand holding her foot. Warmth blossomed from her crotch and radiated through her body. She sighed and relaxed deeper into her nest of pillows.

When he had finished painting all five nails, he took her foot in both hands and firmly massaged her arch and heel and the pads below each toe.

"Mm, that's nice," she moaned.

Aidan finished his massage by running his hand from her heel up her leg but stopping before he reached her crotch.

She whined, "Aren't you going any farther?"

"Not yet." He picked up her right foot and began painting.

"I have needs, you know," she pouted.

With deft strokes, Aidan finished his work then gave her right foot a massage, digging into the tender muscles of arch and heel.

"Oh my god," she moaned as he rotated her ankle, "I should pimp you out to all my friends and make tons of money."

Her eyes flickered open and Delia watched his back muscles move and noticed that his hair was really getting long and shaggy. She liked it crazy wild like that. It was great for running your hands through and for gripping when you wanted to point his head in any particular direction.

Aidan put her foot down and turned to face her. He stroked his hand up her thigh but again stopped short of her aching cunt.

"Go on!"

He regarded her with predatory eyes. "I bet that I can make you come without ever touching your pussy." He continued to run both hands up and down her legs, light caresses that set her inner thighs quivering. "Want to find out?" He traced a wet trail with his tongue up the inside of her thigh.

"No! I just want you to go down on me...."

Aidan shook his head, looking amused. "In fact, move up and let me sit behind you. I'm going to paint your fingernails too."

"What? No!"

He pulled her forward by one arm and moved into place behind her, settling her between his legs. He nuzzled the side of her neck until Delia squirmed, then brushed her hair aside and kissed a path from throat to shoulder. He began to rub soft little circles on her belly. Her clit was crying for attention and Delia reached down to urge his hand lower but he resisted.

"No touching."

"Fine. Whatever. Play your stupid game."

Aidan reached around Delia's body and began painting her fingernails. Every time his arm accidentally brushed her bare breasts, it felt more arousing than if he were purposely stroking them. Her nipples peaked in response.

Delia was aware of every place his body touched hers; his chest and stomach against her back, his legs surrounding hers, his arms encircling her and his dick pressing hard and hot in the cleft of her butt. She smiled at the thought that he was as aroused as she was. *We'll see who breaks first.*

After he had finished painting the nails of her left hand he blew them dry while moving his thumb in featherlight circles on her palm. Then he leaned over her shoulder and kissed her palm, eyes closed and lips parted. She shivered when she saw a flash of pink tongue and felt it lap over her palm. Her fingers curled and she let out a soft exhalation.

He flicked a sideways glance at her and smiled then licked over her pulse point.

Delia suppressed a moan. She could feel her cunt, wet and tender and unfilled. She squeezed her thighs together to try to relieve the aching.

Aidan reached for her other hand. Delia collected her wits enough to decide that she would break his erotic spell. She had some tricks of her own up her sleeve—or would have if she were actually wearing something and it had sleeves.

As she extended the polish bottle toward him, she shifted her ass with a little wiggle targeted at his cock.

He paused and made a disgusted sound. Delia looked at her finger to see a blob of polish off to the right of her nail.

"Quit wiggling," he commanded.

"I'm just getting comfortable."

Delia stopped trying to arouse him then because she really didn't want messy nails or ruined bedding. She waited while he finished her right hand.

He ran his hands up both arms and cupped her shoulders. "You're so beautiful," he murmured huskily into her ear. "Love your neck." He burrowed in to lick it. "Really love your lips." Putting a hand to her jaw, he guided her face toward his for a kiss. Their lips brushed together lightly then with more intensity. Delia turned to face him, wrapping one hand around his neck and resting the other against his chest. She could feel his heart beating rapidly. Her hand skated down over his taut nipple and toned abs. His stomach muscles twitched at her touch but he intercepted her hand before she could grab hold of his cock. "No touching."

"I thought that was no touching me, not no touching you," she argued. "I'm not the one who said I could make you come with just my magic sexy mojo. I want to touch."

"You want to make me lose control." He covered her mouth with his before she could argue and pulled her close. It was a fatal mistake.

Now Delia was straddling his legs with her knees pressed against his hips and her ass on his lap. Her breasts were mashed against his chest and she was aware of her clit rubbing against his dick. She rocked against him until he moaned.

Pushing him back against the pillows, she lay on top of him and began kissing his jaw, his neck and the hollow of his throat.

Who's got the upper hand now? she thought as she spread herself over him like jelly on bread. His breath gasped in and out through his open mouth. He was panting like a dog; he was just where she wanted him.

She kissed across his chest to one hard nipple and bit it. He hissed, "Delia. You're...cheating."

"N'm'not," she mumbled into his skin.

"Yesss, you are." He thrust up against her soft belly.

"Do you care?" she asked, moving from one nipple to the other and sucking it into her mouth.

"No. Not really."

Inside she gave a Dr. Evil victory laugh at his surrender as she crawled up his body and hung over him. She stared into his dark eyes and slowly lowered her cunt to his throbbing cock. She pressed down until he was fully sheathed inside her, then moved languidly up and down, forcing a groan from him.

Delia smiled. Men might have superior physical strength but if you had power over their dicks they were so helpless. She watched Aidan's slitted eyes and open mouth as he grunted out his pleasure, and she felt the mounting exquisite tension mirrored in her cunt. She swallowed hard and closed her eyes, digging her shiny new nails into his biceps and holding tight as she rode his shaft like a carousel pony. Aidan's hands clutched her hips fiercely. He thrust into her again and again.

Her orgasm built until Delia couldn't distinguish where her body ended and his began. Then Fourth of July fireworks crackled through her body and she climaxed with a wordless cry. Her intensity drove Aidan over the edge too and he bucked up hard one last time. She could feel him pulsing inside her as he released.

Delia collapsed and kissed his sweaty shoulder, then rested her head on his chest.

"I could have done it—made you come without touching."

"Well of course you could have," she said patronizingly. "But now I guess you'll just have to try to prove it to me another day."

"Hm," he grumbled.

"You know, if you're very good and stop pouting," Delia

reached up and traced a finger over his lips, "I might let you put a second coat of polish on my toenails in a little while."

"Oh yeah?" She could feel his lips shift into a smile under her fingertip. "Well, if you're very good, maybe I'll let you paint mine."

FENCING WITH DISCIPLINE

Thea Hutcheson

Dan is a tall, well-muscled black man, the perfect complement to my petite, well-proportioned white body. We met at a fencing school. I was just learning and he was already an expert. At first, I was simply attracted to the way he moved. Watching him in action was like watching a cat hunt. His muscles slid smoothly under his skin and he possessed a powerful masculinity that demanded an answer. I decided that I very much wanted to be the one to answer it.

After a few weeks, I asked him for a sparring match. I was so busy watching him move that he was able to score on me several times. "Theda," he said when we'd finished. "You're not focused. You need discipline."

I smiled, wishing he was my fencing master instead of the puckered old man I studied under. Afterward we talked and I asked him out. Dinner was tight with innuendo and sly touching. We practically flew out of the restaurant in our haste to get to bed. The sex was spectacular. I had never met a man so open and willing.

But one night we had a small misunderstanding, and I felt bad because it was my fault. When we came home, he looked me straight in the eye and said, "Get in the bedroom and put on something sexy."

I was surprised because he wasn't smiling. Wanting to make up for earlier by pleasing him, I did as I was told. I put on my favorite teddy, satin with lace across the breasts and pussy. I snapped it closed at the crotch, noticing that I was already wet. Dan walked in and, without saying a word, grabbed the hair at the base of my neck and turned my head up to look at him. He kissed me roughly on the mouth. He tweaked my nipple hard. It hurt and I sucked in my breath. Then I noticed that the pain ran down my belly and turned into a warm glow at my pussy.

I was surprised at this treatment since everything else had been friendly and affectionate. But I was also really excited.

"You are inexperienced. Just like in your fencing, you need discipline; you need a master to train you. I'm willing, but you have to tell me that you'll submit to me. You have to tell me that you're willing to study under me."

He was stroking my ass gently. His touch across the satin whispered over my sensitive skin and I could feel my pussy getting even wetter. "I want you to teach me."

"Say, 'yellow,' if it is too much, or 'red,' if you want to stop."

I nodded.

He bent me over and swatted my ass. The sharp pain went straight to my pussy and the crotch of my teddy was soaked.

He released my hair and looked me up and down. "Suck me, Theda."

I knelt, opened his pants and pulled out his cock. It was hard and thick as I took it into my mouth. He grasped the back of my head and drove his cock into my mouth. I wanted to put my arms around him. He gripped my hair and pulled my head back.

"You only do as I say, do you understand?"

"Yes," I whispered.

"Suck me, then." I could feel his legs and belly tense as he fucked my mouth. He pushed me off. "Get on the bed."

I jumped up and ran to lie down on the bed. He turned to me and took his clothes off. I smiled as I took in his strong body and sleek jutting cock. I wanted to cup his heavy balls and suck them into my mouth.

He climbed in beside me. "Suck my dick some more."

I nestled between his legs and stared at his engorged dick before dipping down to take it into my mouth. He was so big that I was afraid to take more than a couple of inches. As I engulfed his head, he shifted his hips and more dick slid into my mouth. I concentrated on relaxing so I could take more. I wanted to please him by learning to take all of him. I sucked hard and squeezed the rest of his shaft.

"Faster, and squeeze harder, Theda. You're doing fine." My heart soared and I stopped to look at him.

He regarded me coolly for a moment and said, "I didn't say to stop."

I bent back over and worked his dick with a will. I licked it up and down and sucked his massive balls into my mouth one after the other, savoring their taste and shape.

"Enough of the balls, girl. Suck my dick."

Obediently, I ran my tongue back up his length and swirled it around the tip and took it into my mouth. He reached up and pushed my head down, gripping my hair and moving me up and down. I let go of his dick only to rub my sopping clit.

He grabbed my arm before I could come and said roughly, "I didn't say you could do that." He pulled me up and turned me so that I lay across his lap. I could feel his dick jutting into my belly. He reached between my legs and pulled the crotch open. The air played against my wetness and I shivered. He lifted the bottom of the teddy and laid it back over my hips. I wiggled in pleasure.

His hand came down across my ass. It stung mightily and the warmth flowed across my cheeks and down between my legs to throb in my clit. He spanked me five more times. He pulled me up. "Now go back to work."

I knelt between his legs, ass burning. This was like nothing I had ever done before and the combination of him bossing and my submitting was very exciting. I sucked Dan's dick like nobody's business. After a few moments he pushed me off him and jerked his cock a couple of times. I leaned forward expectantly and come sprayed a pretty design across the satin and lace.

He rolled me over on my side and pinioned my legs between his, holding my arms tightly as he put his still hard cock into me. I shuddered and moaned.

"Do you know why you like it this way? Tell me."

I was at his mercy, in his control. I discovered it was a sexy feeling to be held by such manly strength and I liked it. "I like you to fuck me this way because I can't get away. Because you can pleasure me however you like. Because I have no choice."

He rewarded me with a kiss across the back of my shoulder, wet, faintly tickly, with a hint of tooth. It drove me crazy and he knew it. I squirmed to get away and he held me tightly. He reached down with one hand to squeeze my pussy. He had never done that before and the tight pleasure confining my throbbing cunt made me come. I soaked our thighs with my come and groaned as if I thought it would never stop. Finally, I lay content in his arms and we dozed off.

Since then, he's been busy and I haven't seen him. I wonder if he's waiting for another misunderstanding, so I'll have another reason to be meek. Discipline: I really need it. I guess I'll have to arrange for another lesson really soon.

THE LAST GOOD-BYE

Alison Tyler

B e ready for me," Connor said over the phone. "I'll be over in ten."

"Ready?" My voice trailed upward, making a question of the single word, while my mind raced. Ready. I already knew what that meant. Connor had considered our last two weeks together as a form of sexual boot camp. He spent his days packing boxes of belongings for shipping home, saying good-bye to friends, tying up loose ends.

He spent his nights tying up loose ends, too. Pulling the ends of loose scarves until they tightened securely around my wrists... fastening a blindfold over my eyes...capturing my ankles with his leather belt. We took our opportunities wherever we could find them. This was our final weekend together, and he was determined to educate me, to make my fantasies come true.

The night before, he'd surprised me with a bag of supplies from the Pleasure Chest, a red and black paddle, a soft purple suede flogger, a set of silver cuffs. And there were more gifts, ones he didn't let me open yet. He hadn't used any on me. But he'd watched as I unwrapped each new toy, and when I looked up at him, swallowing hard, he cocked a blond eyebrow at me and said, "Tomorrow night, you won't be quiet any longer."

I knew what that meant. I was always quiet. Practically silent. Connor had been trying to get me to open up, to feel comfortable enough to let loose. The most I'd managed so far was a husky moan. I'd never been a screamer. I internalized everything. Tears might streak my cheeks, but I would not cry out. Connor had plans to change that.

While I waited for him, I paced the apartment, clad in an outfit we'd bought together: short black-and-white plaid skirt, silky black T-shirt, fishnet stockings, knee-high Docs. I walked into the bedroom, where I'd set out all the toys Connor had given me. Then I paced again. He'd used his belt on me, but never a paddle. I stroked the flat side, tentatively touched the wooden handle. It was in my thoughts to try the thing on myself, to see what the pain would feel like, when I heard Connor knock.

Feeling guilty for no reason, I hurried to the front door and let him in. He had flowers with him. And a crop.

Jesus.

He looked me over, head to toe, then nodded his approval. The flowers were left to die on the Formica kitchen counter. There wasn't even time for filling a wine bottle with water. Connor grabbed my wrist and led me back to my bedroom, where he sat on the edge of the bed and looked at me. I knew what to do. I understood his expressions now, could practically read his thoughts, but the crop kept me from coming forward. The way it leaned against the dresser made me want to run and hide. Not because I didn't want it, but because I was scared to death. I'd confessed all of my secrets to Connor, over our months together. I'd told him every little fucked-up fantasy I'd ever had. I couldn't hide from my truth, but I had a difficult time facing it head-on.

"Get the paddle," he said. My legs threatened to give out as I walked to the nightstand and gripped the new toy. "Over my legs, girl," he hissed. "Now."

I bent myself into the proper position, felt his warm hand lifting my tiny skirt, felt him watching me. He pressed the paddle against my panty-clad ass, letting me feel the weight of it, before he landed the first blow. I sucked in my breath, but remained silent. It was different from the belt, but not worse. He began spanking me more rapidly, pausing only to pull my black satin bikinis down my thighs, leaving them on me, but baring my ass. The pain intensified immediately, and tears wet my eyes, but I still didn't cry out. I wasn't trying to test him. This wasn't a game. I didn't know how to do what he wanted. Not without sounding phony. Not without being fake.

"What did you think about today?" he asked, taking a break to pull my panties off completely and then herd me to the full-length mirror on the back of the door, to show me my scarlet rear cheeks. He held my skirt up for me, so I could see, and he grinned at his handiwork, clearly pleased with himself.

"This—" I said. All day long I'd thought of Connor and his bag of toys.

"And this?" he queried, cupping my pussy with his hand and giving me a stern look, no sign of a smile now.

I wanted to melt into nothing. Disappear into a silver mist. Over one midnight confession, I'd asked him if he'd spank me... and then, unable to actually voice the request, I had simply put his hand over the front of my panties. "Spank me here...?"

For some inexplicable reason, I was always waiting for the moment when I'd go too far. When he'd give me a disgusted look and push me away. I didn't realize that Connor's own fantasies were darker than my own, went further than I'd dare to dream.

He'd laughed; not mean, not cruel; but still, he'd laughed at me. As if it went without saying that he'd do what I asked. "Baby," he said softly, "I have no problem punishing your pussy."

Ah, fuck me—

Now, he carried me back to the bed, spread me out, and tied me to the frame like the bondage pro he was. He cut my skirt off, cut my T-shirt away, then ran his fingertips over the shaved skin of my pussy. I had only my thigh-high fishnets on now. Nothing to protect me.

"You know you're a bad girl," he said, "don't you?"

I nodded, and then immediately whispered, "Yes, Connor."

"And you know tonight I'm going to make you scream."

Tears started running down my cheeks. I was shivering all over, but I managed to say, "Yes, Connor."

He reached for the suede flogger, and then he looked at me, fiercely, and said, "And you know you need this."

I did. I knew it. I'd known it for years.

The flogger was light, a gentle caress at first. And then it began to sting, the many tails landing faster and harder on my tender skin. I closed my eyes and clenched my fists. But it wasn't until Connor dropped that soft, sweet toy, replacing it with the very lip of his leather belt again and again on my pussy, putting power behind it, that I finally started to give him what he wanted. I could hear the wetness as the leather connected, and I could feel the lake of juices under my ass, and I started to cry for real.

"Open your eyes," Connor insisted.

My eyelids flickered, fluttered, and he doubled the belt and landed a blow on my upper thighs that made me gasp.

"Don't test me, girl," he said, his words matter-of-fact, not a faux threat. "You obey when I give a command."

He did what he said. He punished me between my legs until I came, crying out so loudly, repeating his name over and over like a mantra, knowing that it didn't matter if he was leaving.

Tonight, I was his.

WHAT KIND OF A SLUT ARE YOU, ANYWAY?

N. T. Morley

1. You're on a first date with a guy you really like. After dinner and a romantic drive, he suggests you skip the chick-flick at the local megaplex and head straight back to your place so he can "get to know you better." How do you gently turn him down?

a) "My place? You've got to be kidding—I've got six roommates, and the usual Friday-night, all-nude pillow fight is probably just getting started."

b) "Not a chance—my boyfriend's still handcuffed to the bed."

c) "No way—they just took out the armrests in the back row at the megaplex and I've been *dying* to try it out."

d) "Sorry, pal, but—whew! Five times in the backseat is enough for one night. I'm pooped!"

2. You've just gotten it on for the first time with a new guy. The next morning, while you're both relaxing and feeling great, he asks if you do anal. What's your answer?

a) "Sorry, I used up all my lube with another guy just before our date."

b) "Absolutely, but I'd better wash my strap-on first."

c) "Duh, buddy! How drunk *were* you last night?"

d) "What was your name again?"

3. While you're out to dinner with your boss at an expensive German restaurant, he comments that he's heard around the office he should order you up a plate of jumbo bratwurst. Do you:

a) Say "Well, based on this afternoon's conference, sir, I think you'll recall my fondness for Vienna sausage."

b) Ask him if his wife's free tonight—you actually prefer surf & turf.

c) Demonstrate that it's all true—with your entrée.

d) Tell him "Oh, I was here for lunch; I've already had most of the wait staff. I'll just have a salad."

4. You're playing a drunken game of truth or dare with some girlfriends. You pick "truth," and get the question: what color panties are you wearing? Oh no! You can't remember. What do you do?

a) Lift your skirt and check—were those tigers or leopards that you wore today? Oops! Did you leave them at Frank's or Marie's place? No, that's right; they're still in the alley behind the meat market.

b) Say "I don't remember, but I *do* seem to recall that the little vibrator that fits in the front—Oh! Oh god! Oh yes! Uhhh!—is kinda…whew!…pinkish."

c) Wait until you finish sucking off the pizza guy—last time you picked "dare"!—and then check the chandelier. Yup, you remembered right—pink!

d) Nothing—that bitch knows perfectly well they're still stuffed in your mouth, and if she'd just take off the handcuffs you'd pull off the duct tape and check.

5. You and your new beau decide to videotape yourselves getting steamy. Whoops! You accidentally return the tape to the video store in the sleeve for *Bridget Jones' Diary*. Do you:

a) Go back red-faced and ask for your tape back.

b) Never go back to *that* video store!

c) Head over there with your honey on a slow night—and give the staff a live reenactment in the back room!

d) Send the video store an invoice.

6. Coming home from the store one evening, you discover your roommate getting her freak on with her new boyfriend—who

just happens to be handcuffed to the kitchen table. Do you:

a) Make yourself scarce for a few hours—there's this great bar right down the street, and the guys there are *soooooo* cute!

b) Get mad—it's *your* night to use the kitchen table! (Besides, your catfight last week *really* got her boyfriend going!)

c) Apologize—all they had at the liquor store were lemons, and they were out of salt! Guess you and your roommate will have to lick her boyfriend's sweaty body before each shot.

d) Apologize—to the four sailors coming up the stairs behind you. Guess you'll just have to crowd into the bedroom!

7. You're celebrating Mardi Gras on Bourbon Street in New Orleans. A large group of frat boys start chanting at you to lift your shirt. Do you:

a) Do it, but don't take off your bra. Oops! You're not wearing one!

b) Head up to a balcony to give them a better view—after first making sure that they've got zoom lenses on their camcorders.

c) Tell your mom they were talking to you, but hey—the more the merrier!

d) Tell them they'll have to wait until you're finished blowing your new friend the nice police officer—cops on horseback are sooooo sexy!

8. You write an email to your best friend detailing everything you did with your boyfriend last night—in *excruciating* detail! Oops! You accidentally sent it to all your coworkers, including your boss. Do you:

a) Skulk around the office for a few days waiting to get fired—then offer to fuck your boss if he'll just forget the whole thing.

b) Pretend nothing happened. It's nothing these people don't already know—most of them firsthand.

c) Figure the cat's out of the bag, and send a follow-up email with a link to your webcam.

d) Post it in the lunchroom in case anyone missed it.

9. You're headed for a long vacation with your honey. On the plane, he leans over and suggests that the two of you join the mile-high club. What do you say?

a) "Baby, I'm already a charter member!"

b) "Yeah, right! If you're saying a hand job doesn't count then maybe I'll just take my hand out of your pants!"

c) "Sure, but let's wait until that cute little stewardess is free, okay?"

d) "Hm. So...I guess that wasn't you in the bathroom on the connecting flight?"

10. Your best girlfriend introduces you to her new boy toy. Oops! It's a guy you hooked up with a few months ago. What do you do?

a) Wink at him when she's not looking.

b) Wink at him when she *is* looking.

c) Give him back the two hundred dollars he gave you for "cab fare." The next one's on *your* dime!

d) Same thing you did the last three times it happened— invite them to have a threesome, of course!

Rate Yourself!

Give yourself one point for every *a* answer, two for every *b*, three for *c* and twenty-five for *d*.

What kind of a slut are you, anyway?

10–20: You know, you're kind of a slut. Work on it.

21–40: Are those someone else's panties on the floor, or are you just glad to see me?

41–60: You're telling me you read this magazine *during* sex?

60–249: Have you ever considered a career in public relations?

250: You are a *perfect* slut! If you don't work here already, we want to see your resume! Better yet, come in for an interview—after hours.

ON YOUR BACK

Cate Robertson

On your back now, love. Pull your knees up and out. God, I'm crazy for the smell of you, your musky male mix of heat and lust and sweat.

I'm going to slide down the underside of your thighs, kiss your shaft and lift your balls sweetly, attending to every inch, tonguing my way along that tender skin.

Lift your hips higher and I'll go even lower. I'll flick you with playful licks and swipe your crevice. Without warning, I'll curl my tongue and drive it gently right up behind, make you gasp and moan.

Shhhh. Let me take your breath away.

ABOUT THE EDITOR

Called "a trollop with a laptop" by *East Bay Express*, Alison Tyler is naughty and she knows it. Ms. Tyler is the author of more than twenty explicit novels, including *Learning to Love It*, *Strictly Confidential*, *Sweet Thing*, *Sticky Fingers*, *Something About Workmen*, *Rumors*, *Tiffany Twisted*, and *With or Without You* (Cheek). Her short stories have appeared in more than seventy anthologies and have been translated into Spanish, German, Italian, Japanese, and Dutch.

She is the editor of *Batteries Not Included* (Diva); *Heat Wave*, *Best Bondage Erotica* volumes 1 & 2, *The Merry XXXMas Book of Erotica*, *Luscious*, *Red Hot Erotica*, *Slave to Love*, *Three-Way*, *Happy Birthday Erotica*, (all from Cleis Press); *Naughty Fairy Tales from A to Z* (Plume); and the *Naughty Stories from A to Z* series, the *Down & Dirty* series, *Naked Erotica*, and *Juicy Erotica* (all from Pretty Things Press). Please visit www.prettythingspress.com.

Ms. Tyler is loyal to coffee (black), lipstick (red), and tequila (straight). She has tattoos, but no piercings; a wicked tongue, but a quick smile; and bittersweet memories, but no regrets. She believes it won't rain if she doesn't bring an umbrella, prefers hot and dry to cold and wet, and loves to spout her favorite motto: "You can sleep when you're dead." She chooses Led Zeppelin over the Beatles, the Cure over the Smiths, and the Stones over everyone—yet although she appreciates good rock, she has a pitiful weakness for '80s hair bands.

In all things important, she remains faithful to her partner of over a decade, but she still can't choose just one perfume.